PROJECT MIKE

a novel

John S. Lundgren

PROJECT MIKE

Published by John S. Lundgren

ISBN: 10:0692660100
ISBN 13: 978-0692660102 (John S. Lundgren)
Library of Congress Control Number: 2016908168
LCCN Imprint Name: San Diego, CA

For everyone just trying to find
their place in this world.
Don't be reluctant to ask for help.

PROJECT MIKE

CHAPTER 1

"Hey, buddy. You can't sleep here."

Andre tucked his surfboard under his arm and ran off toward the dark water, looking to catch some early morning waves before work. The young man stirred from his makeshift bed next to the wall of Andre's garage, stuffed a ratty blanket into his pack, and moved along.

CHAPTER 2

Ben got to the gym at 5:45 a.m. His first client was at six. He'd been working as a personal trainer for nearly a year now, since he moved to Hollywood from Arkansas. While he'd been told many times that he was quite good-looking and had an admirably tight, trim body, he hadn't come here to find success in the movies or on TV like so many others. He'd already had his fill of TV fame and had relocated to get as far as he could away from his former life. He was starting over.

Sutton showed up a couple of minutes late and found Ben mixing his morning energy drink. She'd been training with Ben three times a week for more than a month now but knew almost nothing about him. In their time between sets, she had told him about her ex-husbands, her distaste for children, and the job she loved as an editorial manager for a men's fitness magazine. Looking good and being in shape were unspoken requirements of her job. And if she wanted to land Husband Number Three, in this town, she needed a tight ass. At forty-two, she thought she was holding up quite well.

Ben was a good listener, and though she was much too old for him, she had developed a bit of a crush. But Ben had shown no interest in her. Still, she decided she would flirt with him this morning, complimenting his physique and asking about him. Maybe she'd even invite him out for coffee sometime, if he was "available."

"Looking good this morning, Benji; your shirt must have shrunk in the dryer," she said, referring to his chest-hugging, gym-issue uniform. "So, did you get lucky this weekend? Should I be jealous?"

Ben was taken aback by her question. It was so out of character. But he simply laughed it off, saying the weekend had been quiet.

She pressed on. "So, tell me about it. What did you do?"

He had no reason not to, so he replied, "Well, my boyfriend and I saw a movie on Saturday and then yesterday, I volunteered at a food program for homeless youth."

Now *she* was the one surprised. Her gaydar was extremely reliable. Hell, half the guys at the magazine were gay, and all the models were. But with these young guys it was getting harder to tell. The traditional lines had become blurred. Heterosexual, homosexual, transsexual, asexual, omnisexual—who could tell anymore? She backed off immediately.

He wasn't shocked that the boyfriend comment had shut her down, but he was disappointed she hadn't asked him about the homeless program that had become important to him. He let it slide and turned the questioning back on her, asking about the magazine and how she develops story ideas. He was a lifelong athlete and a high school football and baseball star, but relatively new to the business of fitness and therefore curious about all its aspects. While they talked, he put her through her paces, increasing weight and reps to make her pay for the momentary intrusion into his personal life.

Sutton rambled on, talking about the complexities of the magazine business and finding the right balance of "sizzle and steak." "Sex and pretty pictures sell," she said, "but providing real, digestible information is what keeps them coming back."

That's probably true in most businesses, he thought.

They wrapped up the session, and Sutton had completely forgotten about her earlier embarrassment. Ben was a cute kid, and she would no doubt be tempted to make a pass at him again. For now, she just shook his hand and wished him a good day.

As she walked toward the locker room, he thought about what she had shared regarding the magazine business, then grinned thinking about just how sore her old muscles were going to feel tomorrow. He also noticed that, in her trendy yoga pants, damn, her ass *did* look quite fine. He decided to give himself at least some of the credit for that, and his smile broadened.

CHAPTER 3

Alex was moving about the kitchen pulling out tools and the ingredients needed to make himself an omelet for breakfast— eggs, ham, cheese, peppers, milk. He heard a splash in the pool outside and looked through the window to see Tommy begin his morning laps. He decided to make an omelet for Tommy, too.

Fifteen minutes later, Tommy was still swimming strong when Alex brought the two plates out to the poolside table and called Tommy out of the water. Emerging naked from the pool, Alex eyed Tommy's shoulders, arms, and six-pack abs. At only five-seven, Tommy wasn't a big boy, but he had a very toned, smooth, muscular body.

Alex had first met Tommy shortly after he'd moved to LA from Minneapolis last year. Tommy was a local, and they had run into each other hiking in Runyon Canyon. After chatting for a few minutes, Alex had invited him back down the hill to his house for lunch. While Alex was making lunch that day, Tommy had decided to skinny-dip. He had claimed that he just wanted to cool off and didn't want to sit in wet shorts during lunch. Alex had quickly learned that Tommy just really liked to be naked.

Tommy pulled a towel from the ready supply stocked daily by the housekeeper, wrapped it around his waist, and joined Alex at the glass-topped table.

"So what's the plan for today?" Alex asked. "Will I be seeing Ben here later?"

"I'm not really sure," Tommy replied. "He had an early client and spent the night at his place. We haven't connected yet today. How about you? Are you getting together with Andre?"

"No, Andre has to fly to Barcelona this morning for work. He'll be gone for at least a week."

"That guy needs to take a break. It seems like he's always working or flying off somewhere."

"He's got a big job, he's good at it, and he loves it," Alex said. "But he knows how to have fun, too. When I talked to him earlier, he had just come in from a morning surf. He's truly the happiest person I know."

"Sounds like you've become rather taken with him," Tommy said.

"Well, falling for him wouldn't be very logical, given the circumstances, but you might be right. I'd never admit it though, unless he gives up cheating on me with that skanky model Emmy."

"Weren't they already dating when you met him? So, isn't he cheating on her with you?

Alex shot Tommy a stern look, and Tommy hastily interjected, "I mean, yeah, what's up with that bullshit? I mean, she's hot and all, but bisexual? Really? Is that even a thing?"

"Ha-ha, nice recovery. You're asking the wrong guy. My ex-wives might agree with you, though."

They both chuckled and dug into their eggs.

"Mr. Axel?" interrupted Juanita, their housekeeper. In her broken English she continued, "I go to the market now. Everything is on the list you want?" She held up the grocery list Alex had prepared.

"Yes, Juanita. Thank you."

"I go now. See you later."

"Yes, thanks again." Turning back to Tommy, "Her English is getting better. I can tell you've been working with her and she appreciates it."

"Man, I love that she calls you Mr. Axel. Alex is too long anyway, so I'm going to start calling you Ax."

Alex shook his head but resisted the eye-roll he felt coming on. Tommy could be such a kid, and couldn't just accept a compliment when it was offered.

"Hey, I'm headed to Beverly Hills for lunch with my parents. Want to come with?" Tommy asked sincerely.

"Oh, you know they aren't very fond of me. They think I'm still creeping on their little boy, don't they?"

"No, I set them straight on that...so to speak. They know we're just buds, now. We've all moved on." Tommy paused for a moment, then said, "And I think it would be good for you to have more friends your own age."

Tommy winked and Alex shot him another nasty look. He admitted that he was a little sensitive about being more than twice Tommy's age and older than the boy's parents. But Tommy had pursued him—and from the rumors tying him to some of Hollywood's closeted older stars, Alex wasn't Tommy's first "mature" crush. He wasn't feeling too guilty.

The parents were Hollywood people, television specifically, where May-December romances are common and everyone prides themselves on their liberal attitudes. Still, it was probably different when it was your twenty-two-year-old son, he admitted. And he understood why it had caused such a stir when Tommy announced that he no longer needed Daddy to pay the rent on his Hollywood apartment, because he was moving in with a twice-divorced, forty-eight-year-old man. But it was a big house, and Tommy had his own room. No harm, no foul.

CHAPTER 4

"I don't know why I always pack so much for these shoots," Emmy told her assistant as she stuffed another shirt into her designer satchel. "It's three days of posing poolside in tiny bikinis. It's not like I'll have time to go sightseeing or clubbing."

Emmy Ayn was a rapidly rising contender among female fashion models. She'd been discovered as a college sophomore and managed to complete her master's degree in finance while navigating the labyrinth of the modeling world. A mixed-race heritage—her father was Asian and her mother black—gave her a unique look that had become highly sought-after. That combination left her skin a toffee color that looked like a permanent suntan but without a tan line. Because she never had to be out in the sun to achieve this hue, at twenty-four, she had no wrinkles and would likely remain that way for many years. Her genes had also provided her with a very thin frame that helped her look taller than her five-five stature. Her height was complemented nicely by voluptuous breasts and a round ass, thanks to Mommy, and straight black hair, courtesy of dear old Dad. As a thin yet curvy model, she'd taken the industry by a storm. Her goal was to model for a while longer before leveraging her degree and savings to make her mark in the fashion business— emphasis on *business*.

"So you're back on Thursday," her assistant confirmed. "Your itinerary is in your phone. Should I send a copy to Andre, or does he already have it?"

"No need—I told him last night. He's on his way to Spain, anyway. I'll be back long before he is."

Emmy had been seeing Andre for nearly a year. They were both mixed-race mutts, his mother being Italian and his father Mexican. Andre had a swarthy appeal with dark hair and eyes and skin that, while it was ordinarily quite light, tanned very nicely after a few hours in the sun, which made for a very sexy tan line after a day at the beach. She knew he was bisexual and had also begun sleeping with a guy close to his own age. That didn't really bother her—she wasn't in love with him and likely never would be. For now, he was fun to play with and treated her well. And being photographed by the media with a handsome, older guy outside the industry helped keep the creeps away.

"The car is on its way," her assistant confirmed. "Your flight to Cancun leaves at four. First class, of course. Let me know if you need anything else." It would be a forty-five-minute ride from Emmy's Westwood high-rise condo to LAX.

"Thanks for everything." Emmy gave her a big hug.

CHAPTER 5

Ben had been raised in a Bible-thumping family back in Arkansas. In addition to his regular church activities, he'd managed to do well in school and excel in athletics. While he had strayed far from his family and their righteous religious ways, he still believed in the tenet of "service to your fellow man." A couple of months earlier, he'd discovered a group with a mission to help homeless youth become self-sufficient. Twice a week, volunteers would meet to provide a hot meal and clothing to men and women in their teens and early twenties. There was a religious undertone but nothing overt. Ben could imagine how he might have ended up like one of these kids if things had gone differently for him. At their age, he had gone through some crazy shit with his family and contemplated running away. He knew he could relate, so he signed up to help.

At one of his early sessions, Ben spotted a guy named Michael. Michael was thin from malnutrition and devoid of muscle tone. He had scruffy black hair with a hint of gray and a full, dark beard. Despite this, he was quite good-looking. Michael reminded Ben a little of himself before he was packaged up for TV, so he could be married off to a girl he barely knew by his zealot parents for the sake of ratings and the opportunity to spread their skewed beliefs.

Ben was usually good at connecting with people, which was proven by his success at signing and retaining clients at the gym. He tried to make eye contact with Michael as a first step, but every time he'd catch Michael's eye, the boy would quickly turn away. He was on to Ben's game and avoided him for the rest of the afternoon. For the next few sessions

Ben continued his pursuit, and Michael was effective at dodging him. Then Michael disappeared. For the next two weeks there was no sign of him. He was a loner, and the other kids there had no idea where he'd gone.

The third Sunday, however, Michael returned to the program. He didn't look good. He had a cut above his left eye, the white tee shirt he always wore was dirty, and he was limping badly. Still, he managed to elude Ben for the entirety of the two-hour program until Ben caught him at the door as he tried to make his escape.

"Listen, I come in peace," he said as if he were an alien, trying to help Michael relax. "I'm not trying to hit on you or sell you something," he continued the levity, "if that's what you think. You just remind me a lot of myself a while back, and it looks like you could use a friend. I'm a great listener, and if you let me buy you lunch tomorrow, I'll prove it to you."

He handed Michael his card from the gym saying, "If you can access the Internet somehow, you can Google me. You'll find all kinds of shit that might make me feel more relatable. I'll be at Mort's Deli down the block at noon tomorrow. Show up, and I'll buy you the best damn pastrami sandwich you ever had, or whatever you want. Take a chance on me, Mike. I want to help."

Ben hoped he had made his point. He'd felt a connection when Michael had looked into his eyes. "I guess we'll see if he shows up tomorrow," Ben told himself under his breath. He joined the other volunteers to pack up for the day, wondering whether anyone had witnessed his affront on

Michael. He hadn't considered it before, but there might be some rule about fraternizing with the clientele, just as there was at the gym. But then that hadn't stopped him from hooking up with Tommy shortly after they'd eyed each other in a yoga class. Michael had disappeared from the program once before, and Ben had wanted a chance to make his case, rather than risk having him vanish for good.

CHAPTER 6

Working with the kids—and especially having gone through the less-than-satisfying interaction with Michael—had been draining for Ben, and he just wanted a little loving. After he got into his Jeep in front of the church hall, he dialed Tommy from his cell phone. Pizza or maybe Chinese, a few beers, a movie, and then climbing into Tommy's bed felt like the best way to unwind. Because of the light Sunday evening traffic, he made it from Santa Monica in thirty minutes and was parked in front of Alex's. He had free run of the house and let himself in the front door. Tommy jumped up from the sofa to greet him with a quick kiss and a long hug. Alex was there, too, and the three of them shared a bottle of wine until the food arrived.

When the delivery girl came, Alex excused himself to go read in his room so the boys could enjoy their meal and talk. He was really missing Andre and wanted to call him, but it was the middle of the night in Barcelona. Even a quick text was out since Andre slept with his phone and had reprimanded Alex before for waking him. Alex was nothing if not obedient when it came to his romantic partners. So different from the way he behaved in every other situation, where he was decisive and authoritative. Anyway, his book would have to do until Andre came home.

"So, what's going on?" Tommy asked Ben. "You look exhausted, but you seem kind of jacked too."

"I think I finally connected with that homeless kid I was telling you about, and I've got a really crazy, really cool—I think—idea."

For the next two hours, Ben explained his plan to Tommy. Since Tommy hadn't inherited the entrepreneur gene from his parents, the idea of taking on something like this on was kind of overwhelming for Tommy. He could tell, though, that Ben was serious and quickly got caught up in his enthusiasm.

"So, hopefully he'll show up tomorrow," Ben concluded. "What do you think? Should I throw this at him all at once, or do I need to nurture the relationship first?"

"Man, I don't know," Tommy replied. "It could go either way. I guess I'd be afraid of him disappearing again." He thought about it. "My advice is to go for it, but try to establish at least a little trust first. You may scare him off, but that's a risk worth taking. Then again, what do I know? I've never met him. You want me to come with you?"

"If I thought he would succumb to your good looks and charm, I'd take you up on that, but he doesn't have the flair of the kid with the pink hair. He might be overwhelmed if I bring someone new. I sure expect you to be standing by for any news—I may need some cheering up." Ben was now finally relaxing.

"You got it," assured Tommy. "Now let's go to bed."

CHAPTER 7

Back at Andre's wall, the young man was huddled under his blanket. It was a warm night, but he still felt chilled. He'd seen the car service pick up the dude who lived here a few days ago and the house was quiet, so he figured he was safe. He thought about his words with Ben earlier in the day. Being called Mike again, the first time since he'd last seen his brother, felt so odd. But it endeared him, to Ben. Minutes later he heard screaming down the block. Obscenities were shouted back and forth. Finally, a "take that, cocksucker" and a muffled gasp before a "let's get outta here" and, eventually, sirens. No doubt another stabbing. There had been three in the area in the last two weeks. All homeless kids. He rolled closer to the wall, his body shaking in fear. Would he be next? How had he gotten here?

CHAPTER 8

Ben rolled out of bed early, kissed Tommy on the back of his head, and walked into the bathroom. He had to get to the gym to meet Sutton for some early morning abuse. She'd abuse him with her nonstop chatter, and he'd respond with a sadistic workout routine. After a quick pee, he checked his hair in the mirror before running his hands under the tap to relieve his bed head. He pulled on the tee shirt and shorts he had worn last night and fingered-combed his hair again. There was no time to stop at home, but he had a uniform in the car that he was hoping didn't smell too much. He'd dress there and squeeze in a quick shower between clients.

He came out of the locker room, and Sutton was pacing, waiting for him.

"It's not nice to keep a lady waiting," she said.

"Sorry, I got a late start. Ready for a killer workout?"

"Ready, boss."

Ben took her through a quick warmup, then led her to the weight rack to begin with some squats. For the next hour he ran her through a comprehensive routine focused on the lower body while she talked of her week ahead. He didn't hear most of what she said—he was mostly thinking about his lunch date, wondering if the boy would show up, and if he did, how he might react to the proposal.

"That's it for today. Great job. I'll see you same time Thursday, and we'll work on the upper body."

"Sounds good. Thanks, Ben," she said, then grasped his forearm. "Think about what I said. If you want to come by the magazine, I'd be happy to show you around. It will give you a whole different perspective on the fitness industry."

Ben had only a vague recollection of her offer. How had that even come up? Was she just hitting on him again? Even so, he was fairly sure he'd be taking her up on the invitation.

CHAPTER 9

Michael had had no intention of meeting up with the guy from yesterday, but last night had frightened him to his core. He didn't know who this Ben was or what he wanted, but he had offered to help, and right now, Michael felt he needed a friend like never before.

Earlier, he'd visited his favorite public restroom, away from the tourists, to take stock of his appearance and do his best to look presentable. In the stainless steel sink, he did what he could to wash his hair and face. The scratched mirror gave him a view of the cut above his eye that had scabbed over. It was probably going to scar. That could help out here—make him look tougher, give him street cred. The beard had gotten out of control, but he wasn't much interested in shaving it off. If he kept himself from looking like he had when he left home, maybe he could forget about the hell his life had been. Not that his life was so great now. But at least he was away from the people he should have been able to trust.

Michael dug the fresh shirt he'd picked up yesterday from his pack. He pulled off his stained tee shirt and looked at his chest in the mirror. His nearly six-foot-tall frame was skin and bones. The matted chest hair helped mask his exposed ribs, but he knew he was dangerously thin. Other than the church meals he was getting twice a week, he wasn't eating much these days. Before, he'd occasionally turn a trick with a guy to get some cash for food, but since the stabbings he'd put a stop to that—it was too dangerous. It's not that he was gay, he had just learned how to get a guy off quickly, and they were happy to pay up. He didn't know what that made him—lonely for sure...pathetic, yeah...a whore, yes...but mostly, just miserable. Michael pulled on the new shirt. It was far too big and hung on him oddly. But it was clean and didn't smell. It would have to do. The extra length of the shirt helped hide his dirty shorts.

Just before noon, Michael was standing in front of Mort's. He tucked himself into the corner to the left of the door to wait. *What am I doing?* he wondered. Ben was late, and Michael began to get even more anxious. He jumped when he felt a hand on his shoulder. Ben had come up behind him. As Michael swung around to face him, Ben extended his right hand to shake Michael's.

"Thanks so much for coming, Mike."

There it was—he was being called "Mike" again. The handshake lasted a moment longer than normal, and Ben placed his left hand on Michael's right shoulder. Michael felt a peculiar calm fall over him.

"Should we go inside and get something to eat?" Ben asked.

Michael just nodded and mumbled, "Sure."

The deli had windows on the front and down the side. They found a quiet table by a window toward the back. A waitress came by, offering them menus and water, then recited the specials from memory.

"We're going to need a few minutes," Ben told her.

"Sure thing, sweetie. My name is Sal," came her reply. "Flag me down when you're ready. But don't wait all day. And we might run out of the meatloaf if you take too long."

Ben nodded and gave her the thumbs-up.

"So, how are things going?" Ben asked a little too enthusiastically, given Michael's status.

Michael looked at him with a puzzled face and said, "Ah, OK, I guess."

That was the first full sentence Ben had ever heard him utter, but he was hoping for more. It was going to take some work to get Mike to open up. "Let's look at the menu. What are you hungry for?"

It was a warm Southern California day, and meatloaf sounded like the last thing anyone would want (or should be eating), but Ben thought the extra fat and calories would probably be good for Mike, so he offered, "What about the meatloaf? Does that sound good? Or a sandwich? Or a burger?"

"I don't know. What are you having?"

"Pastrami sandwich for me." It certainly wasn't on Ben's normal diet, but he wanted to make sure that Mike felt comfortable ordering something substantial. He could see the boy was literally starving.

"I guess the meatloaf sounds pretty good."

"Then meatloaf it shall be. Let's get Sal back here before they're out of it."

Sal took their orders and they both watched as she walked away. She was headed toward the kitchen where she inserted the written order in the wheel above the pass-thru.

As they waited for their food to arrive, Michael sat on his hands, rocking slightly forward and back, looking down at the table then looking out the window rather than make eye contact with Ben.

"So, Mike," Ben began, "I know nothing about you. And you know nothing about me, unless you did your homework." Ben was waiting for a response, so Mike shook his head. "When I first saw you a few weeks ago, you just reminded me of myself, a couple of years back. It was a time when I really needed a friend, and someone stepped up to help me. Maybe I'm dead wrong, but if that's where you're at, I want to step up for you.

Michael's head was spinning. He wanted to be upset at Ben's presumptuousness, but he was also touched by the apparent sincerity in Ben's words.

Ben continued, "I grew up in a pretty fucked-up family. Crazy religious. So I focused my attention on school and sports. This made me stand out in a small southern town. My parent's best friends were on a reality TV show, and my folks arranged for me to marry the other family's daughter on TV. I was terribly naive—our only dates had been the ones that were televised. We'd never kissed, much less slept together, before the wedding. On our wedding night, I was able to perform, but I didn't enjoy it. Seeing her naked, or touching her, didn't get me excited. We kept up the charade for a few months. Luckily, she didn't succeed in getting pregnant like she, our parents, and the producers wanted. It took me a while, but memories of hiding my erection in the locker room after seeing the other guys naked and a blow job from one of my former teammates helped me realize I liked dicks over, uh, you know." He realized he was probably talking just a little too loud but continued on.

As Ben kept talking, Michael thought, *Ah, so that's it. He thinks the poor kid from the street is desperate and therefore an easy lay. Let's see how this plays out.* He'd done worse for a meal.

Sal brought their food. Before taking a bite of his sandwich, Ben closed with, "There's a lot more to my tale of woe that I'll share with you if you want, but I just wanted to have you understand where I'm coming from. I was totally unprepared for what happened to me but, as I said, I had help. It was a small town. One of my high school teachers became a good friend through all of it. He kept offering to listen until I finally agreed to talk to him. When I confessed I was gay, he said he already knew. That's basically my story. If it's not too painful, I hope you'll tell me how you got here."

There wasn't any conversation for the next fifteen minutes. Michael started gingerly at first, then dove into his meal. First the meatloaf, then the mashed potatoes with gravy, corn and finally roll with butter. He ate so fast he barely tasted any of it. Then again, it tasted so good, he couldn't slow down. Sal kept the refills coming on his Coke. Ben polished off half of the pastrami and all his coleslaw. He was going to decline the doggy bag then realized Mike would probably want it, so had Sal bring a box.

As he was eating, Michael thought about what Ben had told him. That was fucked-up shit. He could kind of relate. Ben was starting to earn his trust, so Michael slowly began to reveal his story.

For the next four hours Michael stopped only long enough to take the occasional sip from his bottomless Coke, which gave Ben few opportunities to inject a question. Ben wasn't sure if this had just been bottled up inside Mike for so long that the dam had burst, or if the caffeine and sugar from the Coke were more than Mike could handle, but he felt like he was getting at least most of the story. Michael told Ben of his father abandoning them. How his mother had remarried. How his stepfather had started sexually abusing him when he was eleven. How his mother had refused to believe him when he finally told her at fifteen, had disowned him and kicked him out of the house for speaking "such vile filth." How his stepfather had persuaded her to reconsider because the boy was just "troubled" and then continued to fuck him until Michael finally beat the shit out of him and ran away when he was eighteen. That was four years ago. Michael had made his way here from Oregon. He had managed to survive on the streets—but just barely.

Ben was caught up in Mike's story. He somehow suspected that it had to be bad, but this was worse than he had pictured. He reached across the table and clutched Mike's clenched hand to comfort him. Looking into Ben's eyes for the first time, and with a whimper typically heard from a young boy,

24

Michael asked, "Will you help me?" as tears rolled down his sunken cheeks.

Just then Beverly cruised by the table. Ben had paid Sal when her shift ended an hour ago. Beverly had taken over the station. "You boys want anything? Otherwise we have customers waiting for this table."

Michael looked down at the table while Ben checked the crowd at the door. There was no one waiting that he could see. He looked up and said, "You know, Bev, we'll take a couple of hot fudge sundaes."

"Coming up guys, and the name's Beverly." She snapped her gum and walked away.

Ben shock Mike's wrists to get him to look up. He smiled at Mike and Michael returned the smile. And out of nowhere, Ben thought, *He has nice teeth.*

Before the ice cream came, a plan was beginning to hatch in Ben's head. Mike wouldn't be sleeping on the street tonight.

CHAPTER 10

Sutton was meeting Franklin for a drink. She admitted to herself that she was attracted to black guys, and he looked damn sexy in the picture her sister, Parker, had shown her. But she swore she'd never do another blind date.

She was trying on dresses in the bedroom of her twenty-eighth-floor Wilshire Boulevard condo. "What about this?" she asked as she stepped out of her walk-in closet wearing a body-hugging red cocktail dress.

"Way too short," came the reply. "I mean you have great legs and all, but I can see your yoo-hoo." Her sister had been joined by Sutton's personal assistant, Wanda, who was voicing her opinion. "Make him work for it."

Wanda wasn't educated, and to be perfectly honest, not very good at her job. Sutton had hired her three years earlier as a favor to a friend. Wanda was supposed to help Sutton navigate through her second, messy divorce. The first divorce had been simple; there were no real assets to divide. But this time there was the house in Beverly Hills, and worse, the joint investment in the magazine—her livelihood. Wanda had probably cost her double the legal fees surrounding the divorce, but she was very loyal, and Sutton had come to depend on her companionship.

Sutton took another sip of champagne before heading back into the depths of her closet to find something else to model for these bitches. Next up was a flowing, yellow halter dress.

"Who wears halters anymore? And yellow, really? It ain't Easter. Let me in there." Wanda surveyed the contents of the massive closet. "I'm coming in here tomorrow and reorganizing this mess," she said. "Shit, you hung things up by color. Can't tell if it's even a blouse or a dress without pulling it out."

Just then she put her hand on the shoulder of a teal blue chiffon dress with wide straps and a deep V. "How this? You've got nice titties; let's show them off."

Sutton paused a moment, waiting for Wanda to exit the closet so she could change into the new dress.

"I ain't going nowhere. Gotta be ready in case this one looks like shit, too."

"Come out here, Wanda," came Parker's call from the bedroom.

Wanda didn't move. Sutton untied the strap of the halter and let it drop to the floor. She stood there in her panties and heels, displaying the naked breasts that commanded Wanda's attention.

"Not bad for your age. Perky. Here." Wanda handed her the blue dress, then returned to the bedroom to retrieve her champagne.

Wanda could be abrasive, but Sutton loved her attitude and candor. And, because it was Wanda's idea and not Sutton's request, by this time tomorrow, the organization of Sutton's closet would make a lot more sense. *Maybe I should give her more credit.*

"That's the one," they both said as Sutton came through the double doors.

"Take a look." Parker pointed to the large mirror in the corner of the room.

"I like it. And it's comfortable," Sutton said as she reached behind her neck to fasten the clasp. "What about the heels? Too high? How tall is he?"

"The heels look great. He's plenty tall, so don't worry. Probably well hung, too," added Parker.

Wanda slapped Parker's shoulder and rolled backward on the bed laughing. As she rolled over on her side, she felt the faux fur covering the duvet and whispered to it, "You're going to see some action tonight, Harry. Don't be scared," and laughed at her own hilarious joke.

A hair and makeup touchup followed. "What time is it?" asked Sutton.

"Five thirty," the others said in unison.

"Oh, I have to get going. Come on."

"I'm going to stay and finish up some things," Wanda said. "Have fun and I'll see you in the morning."

Parker and Sutton rode down in the elevator together to the valet station at Sutton's front door. Parker's Jag was waiting out front already, and a minute later the valet drove up with Sutton's Mercedes.

"By the way, that dress really makes your blue eyes pop," Parker added, receiving a quick hug and peck on the cheek. "Call me later, if it's not too late. Or in the morning if you get lucky."

Parker winked and Sutton rolled her eyes. They each sunk into their respective sports cars, drove past the fountain, and out the front gate.

CHAPTER 11

Ben pulled his Jeep up to the curb in front of Carole's 1950-style hacienda in Westwood. White stucco walls, red tile roof, leaded glass windows.

"This is where you live?" questioned Michael.

"Yeah, here's the story. I rent a room from a very sweet lady. She's 'old Hollywood.' Used to be an actress, pretty well-regarded, I guess, but hasn't worked in a long time. She's very liberal, so this won't be a problem, and she likes having company. But I haven't warned her you're staying over, so she's going to be surprised. She's not home this evening—out with some of her acting cronies—playing cards, I think. You'll meet her tomorrow, and we'll sort things out."

"OK." The prospect of a safe, warm bed for the night kept Michael from worrying about the details.

CHAPTER 12

Alex was circling the driveway at LAX, waiting for a text from Andre telling him what door at Terminal 5 he'd be coming through. There it was.

From Andre: *Door 3.*

His Range Rover negotiated gaps between rental car and hotel shuttles, and other individuals and families picking up loved ones. Andre had stopped over in New York for a couple of days on his return from Barcelona. Alex suspected that it was a rendezvous with Emmy, but he wasn't going to ask. They had agreed to an open relationship and he didn't want to mess it up now by getting possessive. Andre waved him down and Alex pulled up to the curb. After throwing his bag in the back, Andre opened the front door and slid into the passenger seat. He leaned across the console and kissed Alex with an open mouth. The kiss lasted a bit too long, and a horn blasted behind them. They both laughed at LA's impatience.

Alex pulled away from the curb and Andre said, "Great to see you, babe."

"You too. I missed you." Andre reached his left hand across the seat and stroked the back of Alex's head.

"Where to?" Alex asked.

"I'd love to go to my place at the beach if that's OK with you. Does Maggie the mutt have company?"

"Sounds great." Alex accelerated into traffic. "Yeah, she'll be fine. Tommy's home and I told him we probably wouldn't be back tonight. He'll let her out."

"Great." Andre adjusted the volume of the soft music playing through the car's surround-sound system, reclined in his seat and let out a deep sigh. "I'm so tired. I can't wait to curl up in bed with you."

Traffic was light this time of night so they made it to Andre's Venice Beach house in about twenty minutes. Alex pulled the SUV up against the wall of Andre's garage. As he exited the car, Andre saw a blanket stuffed in the corner and knew the kid had been back. He picked it up and briefly thought about dumping it in the garbage bin but stopped himself. As Alex grabbed the bag from the back of the vehicle, Andre folded up the blanket. At that moment, for some reason, he felt compelled to hang onto it.

The house had been closed up for ten days so, it was unusually stuffy. Andre threw open the wall of glass that faced the ocean and the sea breeze rolled in.

Alex said, "Want a drink?"

"Yeah, how about a scotch and then we hit the hay?"

"Water and rocks?"

"You know it."

A minute later, Alex walked out onto the deck carrying two low-ball glasses, ice cubes clinking against the sides. "So tell me about your trip."

Andre took one of the glasses from Alex and said, "Tomorrow, babe. Right now I just want to sit here with you, have my drink, and listen to the waves."

"Sounds good." Alex knew Andre was beat, but he was still disappointed.

They reclined in the double chaise Andre had designed for his father's company, wrapped an arm around each other, and sipped their scotches to the sounds of the sea lapping the shore.

CHAPTER 13

Inside Carole's house, Ben showed Mike to their room. Mike was sure there'd be only one bed, and there it was. Ben was handsome and sweet. This was OK.

"First things first. In there is the shower."

Pulling a pair of black nylon gym shorts out of the dresser and a UCLA tee shirt, he handed them to Mike and said, "Now get in there and don't come out until you're squeaky clean." He gave Mike a big smile, a reassuring pat on the shoulder and pointed to the bathroom. "When you're done, we'll raid Carole's fridge."

Michael disappeared into the bathroom, and when he didn't close the door, Ben grabbed it and pulled it shut. Once the water was running, he pulled out his cell and dialed Tommy.

"Where have you been?" implored Tommy. "I've been freaking out here. Worried."

"Sorry, I just couldn't call sooner. Listen, plans have changed. I've got him here at Carole's with me."

"What?" yelled Tommy.

Ben wasn't sure if Tommy was nervous or jealous.

"Yeah. Things have gotten very dangerous on the street, and he was really scared. I had to do something. He's going to stay here with me tonight, and then we'll figure out the next step tomorrow. This gives me a good chance to see if he's interested in the offer."

"Ben, I don't know about this. You don't know him. He could rob you blind and leave you for dead. I'm coming over there."

"No! He's too skinny and weak to be dangerous. Besides, he's a good kid. Just had a shitty life. We're going to change that. We're going to give him a second chance. He's starting over, like I did."

"I still don't like it. Is Carole there?

"Of course," Ben lied.

"If I send you a text later and you don't reply, I'm coming over there."

"Fair enough. We're going to eat something. I'll send a good-night text when it's bedtime. Love you, Tom."

"Love you too, Ben. Be safe."

Ben walked back into the bedroom and heard that the water had shut off. He had just enough time to change into shorts and tee shirt himself. The door opened, and Mike came out wearing the outfit Ben had given him. His freshly washed hair had been towel dried but was in disarray on top of his head.

"Feel better?"

"Yeah, thanks. That was great. It's been a while."

"I kind of thought so. Hungry?"

"Always." Michael smiled.

Ben flipped on the light in Carole's retro kitchen. The only updates that had been made since she and her late husband had built the house were the professional-grade, stainless steel appliances. Carole had turned to cooking and hosting a cooking show when her acting career stalled. She was a great cook and needed the right tools. Inside the refrigerator Ben found some leftover pasta and a grilled chicken breast. He dropped the cutting board on the brightly colored, Spanish tile counter and chopped up the cooked chicken. In a bowl he mixed it with pasta and popped it in the microwave on high. He then went back the refrigerator and grabbed a couple of beers. He held them up for Mike, asking if he wanted one. Michael nodded, and Ben twisted off the tops and handed one to Mike.

"Here's to a long and successful friendship," he said.

They clinked bottles and each took a sip. The microwave beeped and Ben spooned the chicken-pasta mix into cereal bowls. Sprinkled a little ground pepper and parmesan cheese on top. They didn't talk while they ate.

When all he could hear was the hollow sound of Mike's fork in the bottom of the bowl, he scooped them both up. As Ben was rinsing them in the sink, he asked "Get enough?"

"I don't know. What else have you got?" He wasn't sure if it was the shower, the beer, or Ben's manner, but Michael was feeling much more at ease now.

After loading the bowls and forks in the dishwasher, Ben reached around in the back of the refrigerator, then pulled out a Tupperware container, "What's this? Aye, brownies! Carole's been holding out on me."

He handed the container to Mike, grabbed two fresh beers and said, "Come on, let's go sit out back."

The sun had set, and it was another beautiful Southern California evening. The sky was clear. Ben flicked on Carole's gas fire pit to fend off the evening chill. Over the next hour, they finished off the brownies and a couple more beers. As they looked up at the moon and the stars, Ben asked Mike about his dreams.

Michael replied, "I don't have any." Now Michael was lying.

"Bummer. We'll have to work on that. I myself, have big dreams." They both laughed at nothing. "I'm beat. Let's go to bed." In their room, Ben pointed to the bed and said, "You take that side."

Michael slid under the covers. Ben did the same.

As he was adjusting the pillows, Ben said "I have a proposition for you."

OK, this is it, Michael thought. *What does he want? A blow job? To fuck me? Let's get it over with.*

Ben lay there on his back, looking at the ceiling, his hands behind his head. He didn't notice it when Michael reached across with his hand and rested it on Ben's stomach. Ben was trying to think about how to start his question to Mike and took a deep breath. Michael read that as excitement, so he moved his hand down to slide under the waistband on Ben's shorts. Suddenly startled, Ben grabbed Mike's hand saying, "What are doing? No. That's not what this is about. Man, I'm not trying to seduce you or buy your services. I don't know how else to say it, but I want to make you over." He paused for a moment, "And document it. No, that didn't come out right. Let me explain."

Another pause. Michael rolled onto his side, staring at Ben. How had he misread this? And how the hell was he going to make him over? *What the fuck?*

Ben sat up against the ornate headboard on what he thought had probably been Carole's wedding bed. "Come on, sit up here. Let me explain."

Michael gave him the benefit of the doubt and did as he'd been asked.

Looking into Mike's deep brown eyes, Ben continued. "Listen, I don't have all the details figured out yet. I had to see if you'd even be interested. You're a nice-looking guy, you seem smart, you should be doing great. But you've had no breaks in life. I'd like to help you turn that around. If you're up for it, I want to put together a small group of us to essentially adopt you."

Michael looked at Ben, confused.

As Ben organized his thoughts, he said, "Transforming bodies is my passion. As I see it, you're the raw talent. For the next twelve months, I want to develop an exercise and nutrition program for you that puts muscle on your skinny frame. I think it would make a great feature for a fitness magazine and maybe for a book, or more. Who knows? We'll feed you, dress you, groom you, provide you shelter. You have to trust me though, and I don't think you're there yet. You have to want to do it, and commit, or it will never work."

Michael interrupted, "And then what?"

"What do you mean?"

"I mean after you've transformed me, then what do I do?"

"I don't know. If this turns into something, there will be some money. You'd get a share of that. It may sound shitty, but if nothing else, you're off the streets for a year. What do you want to get out of it?"

"I don't know. I'm skeptical."

"You should be. Like I said, I don't know what it all looks like or who would even be involved. I think I can pull it together though. I invited you here tonight because I decided to trust you. I guess you need to decide if you want to trust me."

Michael nodded, but his mind was still trying to process what Ben was saying.

"You need to sleep on this. We both do. Let's turn the light off. Tomorrow we'll start trying to figure it out. OK?"

Michael nodded again.

Ben reached over to turn off the light on the nightstand. Michael rolled onto his left side to face the wall. He still wasn't sure what he was doing here, but was pretty sure that at least tonight, he wouldn't be stabbed while he slept. As he lay there, he could hear Ben's breath become shallower. He muttered to himself, to God, and to Ben, "Thank you."

Ben heard him.

CHAPTER 14

The dress slid over Sutton's head as she dressed quietly in the bathroom. Parker and Wanda were right. This dress was flattering, although she noticed for the first time the fine lines that were developing in her cleavage from age. "Reality sucks," she mumbled to herself. She checked her face in the mirror. Not good. She wiped off as much of the smeared mascara as she could. Franklin's closet was at the far end of the bathroom. She had to peek. There must have been thirty unmistakably custom made suits. The athletes and broadcasters she met often wore them. They needed them to fit their powerful bodies, but these expensive suits also gave them the much-needed credibility and confidence they craved in the business world. "Everybody needs a crutch." She was mumbling again.

She walked back through the bedroom just as the sun was starting to break over the Santa Monica Mountains to the east. The early morning rays streamed through the wall of glass. Her condo offered gorgeous sunsets over the Pacific, but this was a view she didn't have.

I could get used to this view in the morning, she thought, looking at the backlit hills, *and this one,* glancing to Franklin's barely illuminated, ebony body sprawled naked across his white, one-thousand-thread-count sheets.

"Damn, he's hot," Sutton mumbled under her breath. *Why all the mumbling?* she wondered.

She ran her fingertips across his tight, smooth chest, his large black nipples, and down his flat stomach with just the faintest covering of wiry black hair. He barely stirred. His flaccid dick didn't seem so intimidating now. Time to start the "walk of shame" back to her own place and try to pull herself together before work. This would be a long day. Was it worth it? Time would tell. She wondered whether he'd call her. Why was it always a question of *whether* rather than *when*?

Her car was parked in the driveway next to his satin-black Aston Martin. She thought about how his vehicle matched his skin. The house, the car, the wardrobe—he must be a very successful attorney. Leaving here, she could be discreet. It was back at *her* place where she'd have to deal with the knowing smirk from her valets. Then again, it didn't hurt for those young studs to realize that even at her age, she was still sexually attractive. It had been a long time since she'd returned home in daylight from a night out, or for that matter, since anyone had stayed over at her place.

CHAPTER 15

"Wake up," Andre whispered in Alex's ear.

He nudged the bare shoulder until Alex began to stir. Andre kissed his lips and Alex's eyes opened slightly before he engaged in the kiss. Alex shifted his body and wrapped his arms around Andre.

"Good morning, sexy."

"G'morning," came the muttered reply from Alex.

"Are you horny? It's been so long."

"Someone's recovered from his jet lag." Alex laughed at Andre's quick recovery. "Yeah, it's been too long. But whose fault is that? Stop flying off to Europe and New York already."

"I told you I only needed a good night's sleep. Come here."

Andre rolled over and pulled Alex on top of him. Alex kissed his mouth and down to his hairy chest. His tongue played with Andre's large nipples and he could feel him getting hard down below. The kissing continued down Andre's stomach and his left hand grasped Andre's already stiff penis. Soon his mouth was wrapped around it. He played with Andre until Andre couldn't hold back anymore. After a few minutes, Alex felt the warm explosion in his mouth.

Andre got out of bed, walked into the bathroom. Alex rolled over and watched him stand at the toilet to pee. The stream was tentative, as it often is immediately after sex. He flushed and headed back toward Alex, reaching out a hand to tousle Alex's hair. "Want to go surf, babe?"

Alex wasn't much of surfer, so he knew it was a hollow offer. Andre kept walking past the bed without getting an answer. As he crossed the shag carpet, Alex admired his hairy ass. He had the sexy body of an athlete.

"I'll be back in an hour," Andre said as he padded into the garage to retrieve his wetsuit and board.

It was the second time in as many weeks that Andre had left him unsatisfied. Alex contemplated initiating a conversation about it, but decided it was best not to stir the waters. He could take care of himself, he rationalized.

He masturbated, thinking of Andre's hot body, and let the liquid goo settle on the sheets as a crusty reminder. It didn't have the trajectory it once had. He chuckled to himself and wondered if that was a factor of age or interest...or both.

CHAPTER 16

Ben stirred when he heard the sound of pans being rattled in the kitchen and the yap, yap from Carole's Chihuahua, Cecil. He sat up partially in bed and, bracing himself with his left arm, rubbed his eyes with his right hand. He had slept exceptionally well, and he was trying to make sense of the situation. He glanced to his left and saw Mike still sound asleep. *Good, the boy didn't bolt on me in the night.*

Ben had imagined he wouldn't sleep at all, given his excitement about Mike agreeing to stay after he'd made the proposal. He thought he'd be awake all night, running through the plans and ideas to make this work. Mike looked so peaceful. It was obvious that he had badly needed a safe place to crash. *When was the last time he had slept this soundly, I wonder, or me, for that matter?*

Just then the blender fired up. *I'd better face the battle,* he thought nearly aloud as he pulled himself from the comfortable bed. *I hope Carole's not pissed.*

He didn't bother to check his appearance in the mirror before he walked into the kitchen where his landlady was busying herself with more food than he'd ever seen piled in front of her.

"Ah, there's my little Ben," she said. "You look awful. Didn't you sleep well? Do we have company? Is Tommy here?" Holding Cecil under her left arm, she gestured to the coffeemaker with her right where a fresh pot was brewing.

He headed to the refrigerator where he had a few bottles of enhanced water stashed. *Busted* ran through his mind.

After a few gulps out of the bottle, he looked at her and replied, "Yeah, sorry I didn't tell you, but it was kind of a last-minute thing. It's not Tommy, but it's not what you think, either."

She gave him a quizzical look before asking, "Well, did you boys have fun last night? Or is it a girl? I shouldn't be making assumptions."

This was uncharacteristic of her. She'd never overtly asked him about his sex life, though she knew about Tommy. And it wasn't as if he and Mike had had sex. Then he noticed her nodding to the Tupperware container he'd left on the counter. He didn't make a connection.

"Pot brownies. You polished them off. Must have been some party."

"SHIT! Carole, I swear, I had no idea. In fact, I know I never felt stoned. Slept really hard, though."

"Well, they'd been in there awhile. Perhaps they'd lost some of their zing. When they were fresh though," and she rolled her eyes back and the back of her hand went to her forehead dramatically, a nod to her acting legacy. She set Cecil down on the floor, saying, "Go play." Then she turned back to Ben. "So, who is he...or she? You never clarified."

Ben pulled up the stool to the island counter and began the story. As Carole cracked eggs and chopped vegetables, he told her about the young man in his bed and what he hoped to do with him.

"Sounds risky. Aren't kids like that troubled? Do you really think he'll see it through?"

"We're all troubled, aren't we? One way or another." Ben chuckled briefly. "I don't know yet if he's reliable. He didn't run away last night though. But once he finds out I drugged him, he may never trust me again. At this point, I'm just hoping he remembers what we talked about."

"I'm about to drop the eggs in the pan. I assume you boys are hungry."

"Starving."

"Figures. Well, go get him. I want to meet your *Eliza*."

Back in the bedroom, he could see that Mike had rolled over and was now facing the door. His eyes opened when Ben entered the room. "So this isn't a dream," he mumbled.

"Nope, you spent the night with me. Do you remember it?" Ben said in an attempt at levity.

Michael looked momentarily panicked, wondering what had happened. He eventually said, "I remember talking. You think you can turn me into a Greek god or something."

Ben sat on the edge of the bed, pushed Mike's hair back off his face, making him look a bit like a guy in a renaissance painting, and said, "Yeah, I'm shooting for Adonis."

They both smiled.

"Are you in?" Ben asked.

"I guess so. I mean, it sounds like a pretty good offer for a guy like me."

"Great. I promise you won't be sorry. Now get up and come meet my surrogate mom."

"Gotta pee first."

A few minutes later, Ben walked back into the kitchen with Mike trailing behind. Michael looked noticeably uncomfortable about meeting Carole.

"Carole, I'd like you to meet my new friend, Mike."

Michael extended his hand and mumbled, "Michael" as Carole ignored the hand and swept him up in a big hug.

"So wonderful to meet you, Michael."

Ben wondered if Mike had ever had a genuinely warm, motherly hug as he had felt from Carole many times himself. To him it had a healing quality. He hoped Mike felt that too.

"Come on dear, I've made you boys some eggs."

Ben gestured for Mike to sit next to him at the island.

"Thank you, ma'am."

48

"It's Carcle," she shot back with a grin.

When they were done, Ben said, "Hey, Mike, why don't you go take a shower while I help Carole clean up?"

Michael took the direction, but before leaving the room, turned back and said, "Thank you again Ma—I mean, Carole."

"You're very welcome, dear. Ben and I will take good care of you."

They rinsed the dishes while Mike was in the other room.

Carole said, "You know he prefers to be called Michael, right?"

"I'm betting he's got a lot of baggage tied to that name, which I'd like to leave behind. No one calls me Benjamin anymore. If they do, it brings back all kinds of bad memories."

"He's a fragile soul. Be gentle with him." Their eyes locked. "And to be clear, I'm not looking for another boarder."

"I hear you. No worries. I've got a boyfriend, and Mike and I are going to be spending a lot of time together. I don't need to be sleeping with him too. Anyway, he snores." They both laughed. "No, I'll start working on alternate accommodations for him today. It may take a few days, though. Is that OK?"

She smiled and nodded.

Mike was still in the bathroom when Ben got back to the bedroom. He sat down on the edge of the bed and began sending off text messages to line up their day.

A minute or two after the water stopped, the bathroom door opened and Michael walked out with a towel wrapped around his waist. Ben was now seeing just how emaciated Mike was. His shoulders were bony, chest flat, ribs exposed. There was a slight protrusion in his belly, a sign of malnutrition mixed with the large Western omelet he'd just downed.

"I didn't know what we were doing and what I was supposed to wear."

"Ah. Come on, my boy—let's go shopping in my closet."

As Mike came toward him, Ben put his right hand reassuringly on Mike's shoulder and directed him to the double doors in the wall.

Aside from the chest hair, Mike's skin was quite smooth, surprisingly unscarred, and blemish-free. A good omen, Ben hoped. He was most relieved to see no homemade tattoos as many of the other kids had. Those wouldn't translate well to the image he was trying to create.

"Normally, I think you and I would probably wear the same size, but I'm afraid most of these are going to be big on you for now. We'll go to the mall later, but let's see what we can find so you aren't wearing a towel all day."

Ben found an older pair of khakis that were tight on him since he'd been working hard on his glutes. He pulled a fitted polo shirt off of a hanger, and a pair of boxer briefs from a drawer.

"First, let's see if the underwear will stay up."

Towel still in place, Michael pulled them up his hairy legs and then opened the towel.

"They work. Lots of breathing room," Ben laughed. "Go ahead and finish dressing while I get cleaned up. There are some magazines over there, and the TV's remote is on the nightstand if you get bored. I won't be long though."

A few minutes later Ben was the one coming out of the bathroom in a towel. He was slender but very toned. His own chest hair was closely trimmed, and the extent of his tan was visible from the tan line just above the towel. Michael had to admit, Ben looked good. For the first time since they'd met, he felt motivated to pursue this for a reason other than avoiding another night on the street. For the first time in a very long time he felt safe, and that he might have a future.

CHAPTER 17

Sutton had called her office assistant from the car to push back a few meetings and give her time to settle in after her night out. Walking into their spacious Century City offices, overpriced latte in hand, she was surprised to run into the magazine's publisher.

What's he doing here from New York? I am not prepared to deal with him today.

The magazine and its other satellite media ventures had been doing well. She had turned the magazine, *IMaximus,* into their flagship product, but she was still always being pressured to come up with the next "big idea." Any stumbling on her part, and the conglomerate would likely move to sell it off. That was rarely good news in the media world.

Her iPhone vibrated, and Sutton snuck a peek. Parker was checking in. Sis would have to wait.

"Malcolm, what a pleasant surprise." Hands engaged followed by a European kiss on each cheek. "

"Sutton, dear, I didn't mean to catch you off guard. I was in town for Oscar's Hall of Fame induction. I decided to stop by since I missed you there."

Oscar Dominic, the former bodybuilder-turned-actor-then-politician had been the object of Sutton's wrath since it had been revealed that he had cheated on his wife and her good friend. There had been no way she would have shown up for his accolades. "I was so sorry to miss it. It was a tough decision. but I'm delighted you were there to represent us."

"Come, let's have a chat."

They spent the next six hours behind closed doors as he quizzed her on everything from strategy to the financial bottom line. As the only female head of a successful men's fitness brand, she was a celebrity. Having to deal with this ambush was infuriating.

At 4:15, Malcolm finally opened the conference room door and rushed out, calling back, "Thanks, Sutton. My pilot is waiting. Have that on my desk in the morning."

Fuck you, you pompous ass, was her privately thought rejoinder. "Sure thing boss," were the words that came from her mouth. She had several hours of work ahead of her to meet his request. Then there was her day job that had been ignored all day while she had been sequestered.

"Get the team in here," she called to her assistant. Anyone who had dinner plans was in for a rude surprise. She checked her phone for the first time since she'd arrived. Three missed calls from Parker.

And a text message.

From Franklin: *I had a great time last night. I hope you did too. I'll call you tomorrow. Will you answer?*

A huge smile stretched over her face. She'd heard from Franklin. Sure, it was a text message, but he'd used complete words and sentences, and no emojis. Thorough, as he had been the night before.

A quick reply.

To Franklin: *Yes.*

"Let's get this done," she called out.

She just wanted to get out of here and focus on her own shit. *IMax,* as insiders called it, could have been her life, but stunts like this made her recognize there had to be more.

Everyone filed into the conference room, wearing expressions that made it obvious that they had witnessed her captivity all day. Sutton gave them their assignments, closing with, "Let's get this done and get the hell out of here. Thanks, guys, for having my back."

"Sure thing, Sutton," was the universal reply.

She could be a ballbuster, but they respected and loved her nonetheless.

CHAPTER 18

Alex was still lying in Andre's bed, hugging his pillow and caught up in Andre's scent, when his phone vibrated and flashed, indicating a new text message. He reached across to the night table for the distraction.

From Ben: *I've got someone I want you to meet. Can we come by the house around 11?*

A quick tapping on the phone's screen.

To Ben: *Ha-ha, curious. U got it Ben.* :-)

Alex's feet hit the floor. No time to shower. It was only 8:30, but he had to get back to Hollywood Hills, and the morning traffic would not cooperate. He was done with Andre for the moment and had no reason to wait for him to return from surfing. He pulled on his shorts and tee shirt. His underwear was MIA: Andre would find it wherever he'd thrown it he night before. "Whatever," was muttered.

Passing through the kitchen on the way to the driveway, he grabbed an apple for the ride.

The drive from Venice to Hollywood took nearly an hour. Alex knew to avoid the 10 and stick to surface streets. He listened to the morning news on the radio, then switched to a playlist of his favorite new songs. He parked in the garage and walked into the house, where his excited yellow lab, Maggie, met him at the door. She had her tennis ball in her mouth.

"Hi, sweetie. How are you? Is Tommy home?" he asked, knowing Tommy's car was missing and he was most likely at the gym.

He walked with Maggie into the backyard. "Give it to me."

He wrestled the ball out of her mouth, and threw it to the grassy area on the far side of the pool. She chased after it, retrieved it, and dropped it at his feet.

This time he threw it into the far end of the pool. Without hesitation she leaped into the pool, swam the length and climbed the stairs to return to Alex. He was waiting with a towel.

"Shake, Maggie." She knew the drill and did it on command. Water sprayed across the pool deck and on to Alex.

"I guess that's my shower," he joked with her, threw the towel over her, and began the rubdown. She enjoyed the attention. "Come on, I need a real shower now. Want to watch?"

She trotted after him as he headed toward his bedroom, stripped, and then strode into the adjoining bath.

The shower felt good. He scrubbed off the sins of the night before while also reliving them in his head—the good and not so good. Stepping from the stall, he dried himself off, dropped the towel to floor, and surveyed himself in the mirror. Sure, he was a few years older than Andre, but he'd been considered somewhat of a sex symbol in his youth and seemed to be holding up well, thanks to a disciplined diet and exercise. Sometimes he longed for the day when he could just let himself go, but that day hadn't come quite yet. He was tanned, toned, and trim. The three "Ts." And he was smart and rich, too. Why was Andre losing interest? He had a sudden surge of indifference as he flexed in the mirror. Then a reflection on his current lack of ambition, compared to Andre's. They were on very different paths.

"Fuck him, if he can't relax and appreciate what he's got," Alex said in mock denial.

Alex had no idea who Ben was bringing by, but he decided since it was his house he couldn't go wrong with casual. He pulled on his raspberry J. Crew shorts and black Ralph Lauren Polo. *"Hollywood," or "Hollywood producer"?* he wondered as he took another look in the mirror. They were two very different things. Reef Fanning flip-flops completed the look of, what he realized was, his overthought outfit.

Tommy got back from the gym and wandered into Alex's bedroom.

"Did Ben reach you?" he quizzed.

"Yeah, what's going on?"

"He's got a guy he wants to do a total makeover on, and he's looking for our support."

"What…the…fuck?"

Catching his own reflection in the mirror, he briefly considered whether this makeover was a fashion intervention.

Maybe his look was "Hollywood producer" after all. Then Alex heard Tommy talking again and snapped out of it.

"Actually, we've talked about it. He's really been thinking it through. It's kind of exciting, I think."

"So, what does this have to do with me?"

"I'm not sure, but I know he really wants your advice."

"And he's bringing the guy over now?"

"It came together faster than he expected, so he's kind of scrambling to figure it out. I don't know all the details, but he really needs your counsel."

Ben arrived a few minutes early. He let himself in and, as had happened repeatedly for the last twenty-one hours, Michael was on his tail.

"Great, you're both here. Tommy and Alex, this is Mike. Mike, this is Tommy, my boyfriend, and our good friend, Alex."

Michael extended his hand to shake both of theirs without bothering to correct the introduction of his name.

"Tommy, would you show Mike around the place while I talk to Alex for a bit?"

Tommy pecked Ben on the lips to demonstrate his authority to Mike and said, "Sure."

Leading Alex by the arm out to the pool, Ben said, "So here's the idea. Mike is a homeless kid I came across at a program I've been volunteering for. I think he's a good kid who's had a shitty past and had to run away. I can relate. I'd like to help him turn things around while also creating an opportunity for myself and a handful of others."

He took a breath, trying to remember all the lines he'd rehearsed in his head on the drive over. "I think he's willing, and I can use my training to transform him from a hopeless, skinny kid into a fine physical specimen. Maybe more. I'm hoping you can see that potential and would be willing to invest in the project."

Alex was impressed. He'd always liked Ben and knew of his background, but Alex had never seen the fire Ben was displaying right now. It was the kind of passion for a project that Alex was now missing in himself. "I'm not sure what you're looking for from me."

"Money mostly, pure and simple."

"What about Tommy? He has plenty of money. Why not keep this in the family?"

"You *are* family," came Ben's reply. "Besides, any money Tommy has comes from his parents, and I'm never sure when they'll cut him off. He and I have talked about it and see his role as stylist and photographer. I want your money."

Alex always appreciated hearing the guys sharing his view of them as a family, and he was now even more impressed with Ben's assertiveness. "So, what's the buy-in?" he asked, using the typical gambling term. And this *was* going to be a gamble.

"Food, lodging, clothing for up to twelve months. I'll do the training on my time."

"What do I get in return?"

"That's another place I need your help. Yes, I need your cash. I also need your advice on how to monetize this and maximize the return on our investment."

For a kid with a physical education degree, Ben was using all the right business terms. Alex knew he was in but wanted to make sure Ben, Tommy, and Mike knew what they were in for and were committed. Alex had come by his wealth easily. Sure, he'd worked hard, but wealthy parents with good connections and the luck of perfect timing in the market had both served him well. He was smart and could be downright frugal at times. His second wife even called him a "cheap bastard" when he didn't cave on her alimony demands. But he much preferred to spend his money on people and experiences rather than things. For a man of his means, he had very few toys.

"Let's get those two out here and make sure we're all on the same page," he said.

Tommy and Michael were talking in the kitchen when Ben came to retrieve them. Mostly, Tommy was regaling Michael about his life growing up in Hollywood. Lots of celebrities, drugs, sex, and more drugs, and even more sex. Even the girls he'd nailed before he decided guys were more fun. Ben could tell Mike was pretty shocked by the stories.

"Come on guys, Alex wants to buy us lunch."

They walked down the hill to Sunset Boulevard and the cafe Alex, Tommy, and Ben patronized often. They chose to sit at a sidewalk table that had a great view of the colorful residents of the neighborhood. The market umbrella shaded their faces, but the sun felt warm and comforting on Michael's back. When the waitress came and Michael ordered a bacon cheeseburger, Alex chuckled and said, "Enjoy that while you can, Mike; I'm fairly certain that's not going to be on your list of approved items for long."

"Now, now," retorted Ben. "There's room for an occasional indulgence. Gotta enjoy life, after all. You taught me that, Alex. Right now, I'm just glad he's finally getting some calories."

For the next two hours, the three of them talked, joked, and laughed. Michael was the outsider. He didn't have much to contribute, but he recognized that these three were good friends, they respected and cared for one another, and he hoped to have that for himself someday. Alex picked up the check, as always. He was the patriarch of the group and enjoyed his role as advisor, confidant, and the wallet.

They walked back up the hill. Alex said to Tommy and Ben, "When we get back to the house, I'd like to talk to Mike for a few minutes. Can you two keep yourselves busy?"

Tommy jumped in with, "Oh, yeah."

"Not so fast, Tom," came from Ben. "I've got work to do."

Tommy pouted for a second, then moved on to a new thought.

Michael and Alex disappeared into the spare room used as an office.

"Michael, I know Ben hasn't figured out all the details yet," Alex began. "I think this is a good project—I hope you don't mind being called a project—but it all depends on you. There's always a risk, but I have a pretty good record of picking winning bets. We'll be betting on you to see it through. I know you're trying to figure out whether you can trust us. But I need to know, can we trust you? I want to give Ben the chance to run with this. He's a great guy who came from a fucked-up family. He's figured out how to take control of his life, find a career and love. He'll do a good job, and I'll be here to advise him and support him. I give you my word— I'll do the same for you."

Alex was so much better at taking control in business dealings than he was in his personal life. There, it seemed, others were pulling all the strings.

Michael was both impressed and intimidated by Alex and his obvious success. He was not used to talking to the type of authority figure he perceived Alex to be. He cleared his throat, and with all the courage and articulation he could muster said, "Thank you, sir. I mean, Alex. This is all very sudden and hard to understand. I think of myself as a loyal man. I mean, if I say I'll do it, I follow through. You've helped me a lot to feel comfortable with all of you. Thank you for seeing something in me that I don't feel like anyone else ever has. Sorry, I don't mean to sound like I feel sorry for myself. Yes, I want to do this."

"Good. I believe you. Believe *in* you. This is going to be fun," he said as he shook Michael by the shoulders reassuringly. "Let's go see what those two are up to."

They walked into the living room. Ben sat at the table writing in a notebook, and Tommy was playing with his big DSLR camera.

"OK, Ben. Michael tells me he's in, and I'm telling you I'm in."

"You can call me Mike."

Alex looked at Mike and smiled, then back at Ben. Ben smiled, too.

"You've got a lot of work to do. Let's regroup on Friday. I'd like to see more of a plan, priorities, timeline, and budget. Think you can pull that together?"

"You bet. I've got clients in the morning but can be here by 3:00 in the afternoon."

"Sounds good. Let me know if you get stuck."

Ben had three days to pull together what hadn't even been a concept two days ago. The notes he'd been scribbling were the beginning of what would undoubtedly become a very lengthy To Do list.

"Tommy, Mike and I have to go back to Carole's. I'll call you later. Love you." They kissed goodbye, a quick peck, at the door.

CHAPTER 19

When Andre came back, the house was empty. He was relieved. He'd felt a tension building with Alex, and he didn't want to deal with any drama today. His father had come to LA from their office in Mexico City and had scheduled a lunch for the two of them. Andre was passionate about the business, but Papa took it to the extreme.

After a shower and trim of his trendy facial scruff, Andre dressed in a slim, gray Italian suit, pink shirt with an open collar, and black, Italian slip-ons. Checking himself in the mirror, he looked every bit the talented and successful international architect and playboy he fancied himself to be.

He jumped into his dark blue, 1967 GTO convertible, a nod to the California beach lifestyle he loved, and headed downtown. The sun felt good on his face as he drove east. And the wind blew through his wavy, dark hair.

Andre pulled up in front of the restaurant, advised the valet to be careful with his "baby," and joined his father on the patio. They hugged and shared the required double-cheek kiss. Within moments of sitting down, Papa began to unload his frustrations on his son. Andre's brother, Antonio, or Tony, was messing up. Tony played his role in business development for the firm too loosely, with little concern for expense There was the wardrobe, the dinners and parties, and trips around the world. It would be one thing if he were bringing in new business. Instead, they had missed out on the opportunity to bid on a major project in Brussels and another in New York. They hadn't even been on the radar screen.

Papa appreciated the creative work Andre was doing. He knew Andre derived inspiration from this Southern California environment. That's why he had consented to opening the office here. Papa wasn't saying it directly, but Andre got the gist—he wanted Andre to spend more time in the New York and London offices, and to call on clients more.

Andre was not about to volunteer for that. He was already spending one or two weeks each month visiting prospects and clients. First he needed to take a run at Tony, get him to shape up and do his job. Tony was great at it when he focused. Maybe he just needed an assistant to keep him organized and on task.

Papa looked at his expensive Swiss watch and motioned to the waiter for the check.

"I must go now, Andre. I'll be back in two weeks, and we'll talk some more."

He left a $100 bill on the table, which covered the bill as well as a substantial tip. When they hit the valet stand, his driver was waiting in the silver Maybach. A hug and kiss on the cheek, and Papa was gone.

As Andre waited for the valet to bring around his GTO, he checked his phone. There was a text from Emmy.

From Emmy: *Back in LA for a few. CU?*

Andre replied.

To Emmy: *Busy now?*

From Emmy: *No. What's up?*

To Emmy: *On my way. Be there in 30.*

At Emmy's, the concierge recognized Andre and let him up to her apartment. He lightly tapped on the door, and she opened it wearing a silk tank top, no bra, and short, knit shorts.

"Hi, handsome."

He reached around her, lifted her off the ground, kicked the door shut behind them, spun and pinned her up against it. They kissed passionately. She reached her hands in under his suit coat and scratched his back through his shirt. He set her down for a moment so he could strip off the jacket. Then he grabbed the bottom of her tank and lifted it over her head in one movement. He cupped her breasts and buried his head in between them. She moaned. His mouth went back to hers, and he grabbed her ass. As he lifted her up again, she wrapped her legs around his and leaned back. She was now tearing at the buttons on his shirt to get it open. She wanted to see his hairy chest. Feel it. He set her down again, grabbed her hand in his and led her to her bedroom. He pushed her down on the bed and pulled off his shirt and pants while she lay there panting. Andre crawled on top of her, pushing her black hair back until it cascaded off the bed. He reached his hand down inside the front of her shorts and fingered her gently. Her hands were now under his briefs, and she had his ass in hand.

"Fuck me," she pleaded.

67

He stood at the edge of the bed, pulled down her shorts, removed his own briefs, then crawled back on top of her. He teased her for a few more minutes, making her beg for it.

"Fuck me, now."

Next, he was inside her. He rolled over on his back and she rode him, her breasts bobbing as his hips thrust.

He leaned forward, licking her breasts. His beard felt rough against her nipples.

"I'm coming," she shrieked."

"Yeah. Yeah. Me, too."

Both their bodies showed a momentary spasm. Then another spasm. Then a third. They were done.

She rolled onto her back next to him. Both were breathing heavily. Her hand went back to his chest and rode it up and down as it exchanged necessary air.

He rolled onto his side facing her. His hand brushed her hair back from her flushed cheek. "That was awesome. You're awesome."

"What's going on?" she asked. "I didn't think a quickie in the afternoon was your thing. At least not with me."

"Oh, come on, now. But yeah, I had a stressful lunch with my papa. I needed to let off some steam. Thanks for being here for me."

"What about your boyfriend?" They had an unspoken agreement to ignore Alex in the equation.

"I wanted to be with you," he replied.

"Good answer, if you ever want me again."

"You know I do." He was already starting to get hard again.

"So I see. Not so fast, though." She got up and walked around the bed. "If I'm just going to be your call girl—the girl you call when you're stressed and horny—then that's how you're going to be treated."

She retrieved the silk scarves she kept in the night stand and, straddling his bare chest, began wrapping them around each of his wrists. As she leaned forward to secure them to the headboard, he reached up with his mouth to bite at her dangling tits. They hung just out of reach of his eager mouth. His hands safely tied, she sat back up and placed her hands on her breasts, cupping and fondling them in front of his face. She reached behind her to feel his stiffening rod. Starting at his neck, she licked and kissed her way down his pecs, stopping at each nipple to nibble. Her hands followed down his sides as she reached his stomach, swirling her tongue around his navel. It tickled, and he giggled like a little boy. She went down his right leg, sucked on his toes for a moment, then back up the left leg. When she got back to his dick, she grabbed it around the base and kissed the tip. Biting lightly at it, he flinched. Slowly, she took the whole thing in her mouth.

"Oh, my god," he cried.

Her head went up and down and he worked to match her rhythm with his hips. He was about to explode when she stopped suddenly. He convulsed for a moment but didn't ejaculate. Then, again holding his member in her hand, she guided it inside her as she sat down on him facing away. He watched her ass as it moved up and down. Her toffee-colored skin against his untanned midsection. Her shaved pussy stimulated by his trimmed pubes. The sight of the movement excited him even more. He exploded inside her, and it dribbled down until she finally pulled herself off. Three times in a few hours beat his previous record—and that had been a threesome.

She untied him and they spent the rest of the afternoon in bed, eating ice cream and just cuddling. He'd completely forgotten about Papa and Tony. He dozed off, and she lay there, letting the soft chest hair curl around her fingers.

He awoke at 5:10 p.m. when his cell phone emitted the familiar double buzz of a new text message. He glanced at it then set the phone back down.

"Do you need to get back to the boyfriend?"

"That wasn't from him." He paused. "But since you brought him up, I have a proposal for you."

"Yes, I'll marry you." She laughed and threw a pillow at his face.

"Clever girl. Not that kind of proposal." Cautiously he proceeded. "Would you ever consider a three-way," pause, "with Alex and me?" The three orgasms had inspired and emboldened him.

Good thing her feelings for him were strictly carnal. That kind of question following the afternoon they'd just spent would kick most girls in their gut. But Emmy was intrigued. She'd had a three-way before, but with another girl. Could she hold the attention of both of them, or would she lose them to each other? "Seriously? You want to not only introduce me to your mister, but also have sex with him and worse yet, watch you have sex with him? Are you insane?"

He knew it had been risky to ask, but he thought if the answer was no, she'd just say so. He didn't think she'd be incredulous. She was pretty adventurous, sexually. She knew Alex was in the picture. This wasn't exactly coming from left field.

"Gotcha." She laughed. "I'll admit, I never thought it would be an option, but yeah, I'd consider it. Under the right circumstances and by my rules. Is he on board?"

Now it was his turn to toss a pillow her way. "Don't know. I haven't asked him. Things have been a little strained lately. This could help or blow up in my face. He's been married twice, to women, so he knows how your…well let's just say he knows the terrain. And he's handsome, too, so I think you'd enjoy it. I know I would."
"Well, you ask him then and get back to me. Are we having dinner, or do you have to go?"

"Rain check? I really should check in on things at work." He located his black briefs on the floor and slipped them on. "Papa's down on Tony. I don't need him pissed at me too."

He finished dressing while she put her shorts and tank back on. A glance in the mirror to finger-comb his tousled hair, and he was ready.

Andre leaned down to kiss her and said, "Thanks for a great afternoon. Let's do this again soon."

"I'll check my dance card."

And he was gone.

CHAPTER 20

Back at Carole's, Ben and Mike changed into their shorts and tee shirts and crawled onto the bed…"What was the last book you read?" quizzed Ben.

Mike's reply didn't come quickly enough, so Ben reached over and pulled a book from the cubby in the nightstand and handed it to Mike.

"Check this out. Alex gave it to me. It's become the mantra I live by."

Live Like a Fruit Fly, by Gabe Berman. Mike started to read. Page 2, *"You are dying."* Mike was hooked.

Ben went to work. He had a lot to do before Friday. On the MacBook he had propped up on his lap, he typed:

—Before photos
—Grooming: hair, nails, beard
—Shopping
—Housing
—Nutrition plan
—Workout plan
—Media options: magazine, book, Internet, video
—Budget
—ROI
—More to come

Next, he had to think through the timeline. He knew he had Tommy's support to help with the photos, spa, and shopping. Those could be controlled. He'd manage the nutrition and workout. The wild cards at this point were housing and budget. What was Alex thinking? He had a lot of money, and he was smart. What would he be willing to invest in this? What would he be looking for in return?

"Mike, help me here."

Mike was halfway through *Fruit Fly*. The boy was smart, too.

"What's up?" he said, eagerly leaning in to look at Ben's list.

"Here's what I have so far. What do you think? Anything obvious missing?"

"I hope nothing is missing, it sounds daunting."

"It will be exhausting for you, for sure, but you only have to worry about this one line." Ben moved the cursor the to line saying, "Workout plan."

That was it for the night—they were both beat. He had forgotten to call Tommy, but he sent him a quick text.

To Tommy: *Sorry T. Got caught up in the plan. Talk to you tomorrow. Love U.*

"Are you doing OK?" Ben asked Mike.

"Just living like a fruit fly, I guess. Thanks for everything, Ben. This has been great day. You have really nice friends. Two nights in a row in a comfortable bed. I don't know how I got here, but I'm not leaving willingly."

Ben leaned in to hug Mike and Mike returned it pulling him close. They rolled onto their backs and Ben turned off the light.

"Hey, can I ask you a question?" asked Mike quietly.

"You just did." There was a pause. "Sorry, bad joke. Sure."

"Have you ever thought about killing yourself?"

This alarmed Ben. Reading *Live like A Fruit Fly* should be having the opposite effect. But he had committed to being honest with Mike, so he answered, "Yes. But I think everyone probably has at one point. Have you?"

"No, not really."

"That's great. Hard to believe, given what you've been through. You've got a strong survivor gene, I guess. Stronger than mine at least."

"What happened with you?"

Staring at the dark ceiling, Ben began, "I was pretty depressed about what was happening with my life. Figuring out I was gay was not easy to accept. And I was throwing away the only life I knew. I had to get out. But I couldn't see a way forward. Anyway, my teacher friend stayed in my face and could tell I was unhappy. He confronted me about it. Asked me straight out if I was suicidal. I wanted to lie to him but couldn't. Then he put it into a new perspective for me. He told me to imagine the headline—Reality Cast Member Kills Self. I'd be a headline for one day maybe. Who does that help? It was sobering. Then he told me to imagine a different headline. One where I'd be mourned for the good I had done in this world, people I had influenced, loved. A legacy that could live on. I don't think I'm particularly vain, but that headline meant a lot to me. I never thought about it again."

Ben sniffled. The memory had made him cry to himself. After this conversation, the realization of how much work he had to do, and without the benefit of Carole's "special" brownies, tonight's sleep would not be as sound as the last. Mike was asleep almost immediately and began to lightly snore. It was more amusing than annoying to Ben. It was a good sign that Mike was comfortable with him and this made him smile. For the next hour, Ben stared at the dark ceiling, his mind racing, until he finally nodded off.

CHAPTER 21

Ben spent the rest of the week working at his job of training clients. In between paid sessions, he developed nutrition plans and workout routines for Mike, while also squeezing in his own workouts. At night he talked to Tommy and Mike about the overall plan, in order to prepare for Friday's meeting with Alex. His personal drive had served him well in his achievements in high school and athletics. Just as then, he was driven now. This had to be right. He needed Alex. There was no Plan B.

Tommy set up a makeshift studio in Alex's garage with lights and a backdrop. This is where he'd be taking all the progress pictures for the project. Tommy was excited to have a real role. He'd gone back to review the textbooks from his photography classes, looking specifically for a refresher on portraits He'd gotten good reviews for the portraits he'd taken for the class, but that was a few years ago. This was important to him, to them, and he didn't want to just wing it.

Thursday afternoon the three of them gathered for the "before" shots of Mike.

"Ben, what are you thinking about for wardrobe?"

"Well, I guess let's try it with just underwear. Mike, will you lose the shorts and shirt, please?"

Mike complied. He had been pulling from Ben's closet all week, so everything was still loose on him, including the gray boxer briefs.

77

"Well, baggy is one way to go," joked Tommy. "But I think we should try to shoot for something a little more, uh, sexy."

"You're right, Tom. My stuff is too big, and until Alex opens the check book, we can't buy anything. Let's see if something you have will fit better. How about some gym shorts? Can you grab something?"

Mike was a little uncomfortable standing in the garage in his, or rather, Ben's, underwear. He shifted from foot to foot.

"Get used to it, bud. Where you're going, there won't be a lot of clothes."

"It's not that. I just know how scrawny I look...compared to you and Tommy."

"That's the program. To change how you look and feel. Build your confidence. Ultimately we're going to help others see how they can change themselves for the better. You're the guy who's going to show them what's possible."

Tommy came back with a few options, which Ben rifled through.

"Let's try a couple of different things. I think we want to have the same look throughout the series. As Mike adds muscle mass, these won't fit for long so we need to know we'll be able to match it in larger sizes."

"The black compression shorts are pretty safe then. They're basic and pretty universal."

"OK, let's see how they look. Mike, would you change into these?"

Mike looked around for someplace discreet and stepped behind the backdrop. A second later he was back in front. Tommy and Ben both looked him over. The shorts were tight.

"Mike, turn around for us."

He did. His ass and hips were flat. The only contour on his body came from the bulge in front, which the tight shorts accentuated nicely. Ben and Tommy looked at each other, surprised to see for the first time the size of Mike's package. They were impressed.

"Looks good."

There was no mirror. Mike would have to trust their judgment.

"First thing I want to do, though, is get your measurements."

Ben had the tape measure and calipers. With the tape, he measured Mike's neck, chest waist, hips, thighs, and upper arms. Mike was ticklish and squirmed through much of the process. With the caliper it was skin folds on his pecs, stomach, upper arms, and thighs. This was a good test to check body fat. As expected, Mike had almost none. Fortunately, for their purposes, he didn't have much for muscle mass either.

"OK, Tommy, let's get some shots."

Tommy took over the direction. "Mike could you step on the 'X' in front of the curtain and face me? Stand up straight. Now flex your arms, you know, show your biceps."

There wasn't much there. The camera clicked in rapid succession.

"Now turn to your left."

Click, click, click.

"Now your back. Flex again."

Click, click, click.

"Now to your right."

Click, click, click.

"Is that it for this outfit, Tommy?" asked Ben.

Tommy nodded.

"Let's see what the black gym shorts look like."

Mike pulled them on over the compression shorts and they repeated the turn and click process.

"I've got more shots left on the memory card. Is there anything else you'd like to try, Ben?"

"Ah, yes. Mike, I promise we won't publish or distribute these, but I'd really like to capture images of you wearing nothing. Would you be OK with that?"

Mike didn't say a word. He just reached under the waistband and pulled down the shorts until they fell to the floor. He stepped out of them, then asked, "Same poses?"

For a guy who had just sought a discreet place to change, he was suddenly showing surprising boldness. Ben had no idea what he was going to do with these last shots, but he knew he'd regret it if he didn't capture them. And now the guys could see the source of the bulge. Mike's dick, though not long, was as thick as his skinny forearm. So that was the object of stepdad's lust...*the asshole*.

Click, click, click.

"How'd we do, Tommy? Is that a wrap? Do we have what we need?"

"For the stills, yes. Are we going to do the video interview tomorrow night?"

"After Alex gives us the go ahead, yes."

Mike pointed to his clothes stacked to the side and looked to Ben silently asking if he could get dressed.

"Oh, sorry Mike. No more nakedness...today. Go ahead and get dressed."

CHAPTER 22

Sutton met up with Franklin after work. Over martinis, she shared, "Work has gotten intense this week. I think they're trying to push me out."

Always the attorney, Franklin asked, "Do you have a contract?"

"Of course, but I know there are always loopholes."

"If you want, I'll take a look at it."

She reached across the table and clutched his hand. She appreciated his concern and might just take him up on his offer, although her own attorney was already doing just that. But right now she wanted to direct her attention—and his—elsewhere.

"Enough of my week. Tell me about yours."

"I signed a new client. Confidentiality agreements forbid me from telling you who, but you'll know soon enough if you watch the news."

She knew he was intentionally distracting her focus. She laughed and squeezed his hand tighter. She then leaned in and kissed him. "I'm right next door. Come up for a night cap?"

"I was hoping you'd ask. You're really special, Sutton. Fuck them if they don't see it. I do."

She melted and they were off.

CHAPTER 23

The time stamp on his phone was 11:30 p.m., and the vibration indicated Ben was receiving a text message. He squinted at the bright screen as he read:

From Sutton: *Getting laid. No show in a.m.* :-)

He rubbed his eyes and looked over at Mike. The boy hadn't stirred. He was sleeping like a baby as he had all week. He didn't understand the importance of tomorrow's meeting with Alex. Ben feared Carole was growing impatient with Mike's presence. Maybe he was just being paranoid, but if Alex didn't buy in, they might both be out on the street. Sutton's cancellation gave Ben an extra hour to prepare.

Right now he needed to sleep, though. He pulled the comforter up over his shoulder and shifted until his back unwittingly met up with Mike's. They'd gotten quite comfortable together. Ben was going to miss this if Alex bought into the plan. "Not *if, when*. Have some confidence, man," he whispered to himself.

CHAPTER 24

Now it was time for Franklin to do the walk of shame. But there was no shame in having spent the night with Sutton. He leaned over the bed and kissed her.

Damn, she'd wanted to make him breakfast, even reviewing in her head what she might have the refrigerator. As she stirred, he said, "Gotta go, Sutton. I've got an early meeting. You're amazing. Call you later?"

She pulled him in for another kiss on those full, sensuous lips. "I can't get enough of you." *Too vulnerable?* Fuck, was she falling for him already? She was still groggy.

"I feel the same. Bye, sweetie."

As he walked away, she couldn't help but stare and think how that suit was molded to his round ass. It was well worth whatever it cost.

CHAPTER 25

Ben got the rare opportunity to sleep in. And he needed it. The sun was up when his eyes finally opened. Mike was lying next to him, playing a video game on his old, cracked phone.

"I didn't know whether I should wake you. Don't you have a client at six?"

"I was supposed to, but she cancelled late. Thanks, though."

He reached over to hug Mike.

"I'm back-to-back from eight to twelve, though, and then I'll swing back here to pick you up. We can grab lunch, then head over to Alex's."

"I was hoping I could come with you to the gym. You know, since I'm going to be spending a lot of time there. I want to see what I'm in for."

"Oh, OK. Sure. Let's get you oriented. We don't have much time. We can shower there."

He didn't know what Mike was going to do for four hours while he was busy with his paying clients, but at ten minutes before eight, Ben was pulling into the parking garage with Mike at his side. Ben swiped his card at the desk and signed Mike in as a guest. He showed Mike around the club and the locker room with its amenities. Maybe Mike could kill some time at the pool or in the sauna or Jacuzzi.

"OK, you're on your own. I'll check in with you between sessions."

Mike was discreet, but Ben noticed him hovering, watching his training method. *As long as he wasn't getting in the way,* he thought, *that's OK. And good for him, for taking an interest.*

During the second hour, Mike disappeared. Ben found him after his last client, reading in a shaded area out by the pool.

They both showered, dressed, and headed to lunch.

Tommy joined them, and they reviewed the presentation. Ben had used the presentation software on his MacBook to assemble a slide show. He'd had five copies printed at the office supply store. They were spiral-bound. He pulled three copies from his bag to show them.

"Impressive," said Tommy. "Where'd you learn to do this?"

"Ha-ha, I watched a YouTube video on making presentations asking for money. You can find anything there. This is what it said to do."

It was a bit like the blind leading the blind. Now, Tommy wished he had paid more attention to his parent's business dealings, rather than just spending their money and flirting with their clients. They were all in over their heads, and they knew it. They were counting on Alex being a sympathetic audience.

Ben began to go through how he saw it playing out. He would do most of the talking. Tommy's primary role was to share the "before" photos he'd taken and jump in if necessary to support Ben. Mike had a silent role unless asked a specific question. At 2:30, they left the restaurant and headed up the hill.

The trio walked into the empty house a few minutes before three. Tommy volunteered to take the printed copies of the presentation to the dining table they'd be using for the meeting. They had no other media, but Tommy would get some bottles of water from the fridge in case they got thirsty. If they'd been pitching something other than fitness, he imagined it might be cocktails by the pool, just like mom and dad routinely did.

"Ben, can I talk to you?" asked Mike.

He looked at Mike. A slight panic ran through him. Was Mike getting cold feet?

Suppressing his anxiety, he replied, "Sure. What's up?"

They stepped outside.

"When we first started talking..."

Oh, oh. Shit.

"...you said I needed to figure out what I wanted. What would motivate me to see this through?"

"Yes." *Fuck, fuck, fuck.*

"Well, I think I know what that is."

"OK, what?" he managed to verbalize. *Don't you dare ask for cash,* was what he was thinking.

Mike held up the book he'd picked out of Carole's bookcase and had been reading, *Trump: The Art of the Deal.* "I want to go to college."

"Really?"

"I know you're going to have me at the gym, working out a lot. But there are a lot of hours in the day. I want to spend that time learning. I want to study business. Make this whole experience around asking for money and building something that makes money not so much of a mystery. Maybe I can get a job to help pay for it."

Ben was blown away. This destroyed the presentation and budget proposal they were about lay on Alex, but he was so impressed with Mike right now, he didn't care. His foolhardy Plan B of bankrolling this himself was no longer an option. He was going to make this happen for himself, and Mike. He had to convince Alex to pay for school, too. Training, school, and a job. Sure, a lot of young people did that. But he was afraid the fitness piece would take third place. That wasn't an option if this was to succeed.

"I'm so proud of you right now, I just have to hug you," he said, and he did. "OK, I'm going to work this into the presentation on the fly. If Alex asks you why you want to go to school, you tell him exactly what you just said to me. By the way, I wouldn't reference Donald Trump as your influence for this around Alex. He's not a fan. And it's not just because of his reality show—but that didn't help." Ben winked.

Mike nodded, and hoped he hadn't just asked for too much. While his confidence had been slowly growing, it didn't take much to make it waver again.

Alex came through the door and dropped his car key into the bowl.

"Hi guys." He glanced over at the table and said, "It looks like you're ready. Should we sit down?"

They all took a chair, except Ben. As the presenter, he wanted to command Alex's attention by standing. He began by thanking Alex for the opportunity to present, as the video had instructed him. For the next forty minutes, he went through each page in his deck. It was rough, but still much more complete than Alex had expected. Ben was doing a good job of staying on topic. He was prepared but not over-rehearsed. They went through the mission and goal, action plan including the first few weeks of exercise programming and nutrition. Next they covered benchmarks and contingencies. Then they got to budget. Ben's budget was really quite modest. He'd included gym fees, a clothing, grooming, and food allowance for Mike, as well as transportation—a one-year lease on a compact car. Alex looked down the list and was puzzled at the lack of any housing expense.

"Where's he going to live?"

"My place doesn't have space for him to stay long term. We think he needs some infrastructure—a family, if you will. I think the best place for Mike to stay is here with you and Tommy. Convert the office into his room."

That had taken some guts to get out. Alex raised his brows in feigned surprise and looked toward Tommy who was nodding in agreement.

"OK. I'm not saying yes, but continue. What do I get for my investment?"

Ben directed him to turn the page where he had outlined the various sources of income that he'd identified. It was heavily social media-oriented with YouTube videos documenting the program. He had identified the possibility of turning it into a book or a magazine series. The next slide contained a list of the media channels and possible revenue associated with each. It was a shot in the dark.

"Maybe even TV," Tommy blurted. "I've got connections, you know."

Ben shot Tommy a dirty look for interrupting the flow. He was stumbling a bit now and finally said, "That's where we really need your counsel."

"I agree there's opportunity here. OK, I can work with you to flesh this out some more. But please recognize that in business, the investors always get paid back first."

He was right of course. But it still stung to know they had a big hurdle before they'd see any of their work pay off personally.

"There's one more thing," Ben said somewhat feebly. He took a breath and more assertively continued, "It's compensation for Mike. In lieu of being paid a salary for his time and effort, he'd like to use the time between training to attend college. He wants to study business."

Ben took a deep breath to avoid fainting, and looked to Alex for a reaction. Alex looked away from Ben and toward Mike. He smiled and then looked down at his vibrating phone.

"Sorry guys, I need to take this." As he walked out to the back yard, they could hear him say, "Hi. How've you been?" and "I'm so sorry" before he faded out.

"Fuck," mumbled Ben. "I totally fucked the whole thing up."

"No, you didn't," comforted Tommy. "Sorry about the TV comment, but I was caught up in the moment. And I think Alex was too." He knew Ben was understandably wary of reality TV. His favorite line was "There's nothing real about reality TV."

Mike just looked at both of them, trying to comprehend all of this. Alex seemed engaged to him, and the whole plan seemed to make sense. Regardless, he was grateful that Ben had made the plea for college.

Alex finished his call and walked back into the house. Rather than stopping at the table he continued down the hall past

Tommy's room to the office. A minute later he came back carrying an easel, flip chart pad, and markers, from his long-past days in Corporate America.

Alex gestured to the set up. "Sorry, old habits die hard." As Alex began writing on the pad, he continued, "Here's where you guys messed up."

Ben's heart sank.

"I appreciate how conservative you were with your budget. But you totally discounted your own time and effort. What Ben, are you going to work for free? And Tommy, you too? At least Mike is thinking like a business guy. And I love that you so understand the value of education that you'd ask for that in lieu of a paycheck. Remember I said that the investor gets paid back first. Well, your time, energy, and wherewithal is your investment in this gamble. And the minute this starts paying back, you need to be getting paid too. My money isn't what's going to make this successful. It's you guys. You've got my money. I'm in. I'll bankroll this because you've proven to me just how passionate you all are about making this happen. Who knows how this will turn out? But I'm willing to bet on you. I couldn't be more proud."

Ben stepped forward to shake Alex's hand. Alex grabbed it and pulled him in close for a hug. Then he motioned to the others, "Come on, group hug."

"Let's drink to a successful venture," and Alex turned to the bar fridge for a bottle of champagne.

The cork was popped. Clink, clink, clink, clink.

"Cheers," from all.

"First things first—Tommy, here's my AMEX. You and Ben take Mike out tomorrow and get him some clothes that fit. And how about a haircut? I'll get working on converting the office into a bedroom for you. I don't know where I'm going to store my easel and pad." He chuckled. "You should have your own space to sleep and study sometime next week."

"Thanks so much, Alex. You won't be sorry," said Ben.

"I know I won't. I've got to go. Tommy, can you take care of Maggie?"

"Of course."

"You guys have a great night. Celebrate."

Alex picked up his keys up from the bowl and was out the door. Driving down the hill, then turning west on Sunset, as the sky to the west turned orange, violet, then black, he thought about what a good job his three young friends had just done.

CHAPTER 26

The call had been from Andre. It had been a hard few days, but Alex was determined to wait for Andre to call him. Now he was on his way out to the Venice beach house for a long awaited reunion. Friday evening traffic on the 10 would be horrible. He expected that it would take at least an hour. He listened to some classic Bruce Springsteen and reflected on where he was at in his life.

When Alex got to the beach he found Andre on the back deck, smoking a joint. Andre was reclining on the double chaise so Alex joined him there. Andre offered up the joint and Alex took it. He wasn't a fan of pot or other drugs but indulged occasionally, accepting Andre's argument that it's "better than drinking, because it doesn't make you fat." His concern was that with Andre's personality, this could be a gateway drug. He'd never witnessed it but was fairly certain Andre had at least experimented with other substances.

The pot relaxed them both and they spent the evening talking, kissing, and enjoying the sound of the waves against the black horizon. The only interruption came when the pizza was delivered. Alex thought, *The pot doesn't make you fat, but the pizza and beer you crave after it sure could.* He chuckled to himself as he inhaled the first slice.

The two men ended up spending all day Saturday together. They visited the flea market, had lunch and even a movie later in the day. Andre held his hand. It was more romantic than Andre ever been with him, thought Alex. Was this his way of apologizing?

Later, in bed, Andre faced him to say that he had to go to Mexico City and London for a week or two, to check in with the company's offices.

"My brother is fucking up. I have to go figure out what's going on, repair some damage with staff and clients, and get him to shape up."

"I'll miss you."

"Me too I'd ask you to come along, but there's not going to be any time for fun."

Alex was disappointed but understood. It had been a great weekend, and he had to restrain himself from getting possessive. But damn, this was nice. Why couldn't it always be like this? He was frustrated, but encounters like this happened just often enough to keep him interested.

"When I get back though, I've got a surprise."

"What?" Alex asked eagerly, like a child.

"No, not until I'm back. It's a surprise, but I think we're both going to like it. A LOT!"

The curtains fluttered in the ocean breeze, creating ghostly shadows in the moonlight, as they both drifted off to sleep. Safe in each other's arms, neither stirred at the sound of the distant siren.

CHAPTER 27

Ben had expected Tommy would be upset when he'd told him that he and Mike were headed back to Carole's. Ben was a regular visitor to Tommy's bed and this week had been quite a departure. But Tommy also appreciated the quiet. He knew things were going to get a lot busier around this place once Mike moved in. He was perfectly fine hanging out by the pool with Maggie. It was the first opportunity he'd had in a week to drop his shorts and fiddle around with his camera. Within an hour, there were a few dozen naked selfies on his memory card.

Saturday morning, Tommy was at Carole's house to pick up the boys. She insisted on feeding them all breakfast before letting them out the door. She didn't know Tommy well, but she liked him. His lighthearted attitude was a contrast to Ben's focus. She noted that Ben eased up when Tommy was around. Tommy made him smile.

"Bacon and eggs, breakfast of champions," she said, setting a platter of each down in front them at the patio table. They were all a little groggy from the second bottle of Alex's champagne that they had finished off the night before.

"This is awesome, Carole," said Tommy. "Thanks so much."

"Cheers," Ben said as he hoisted his glass of orange juice toward Carole.

Thirty minutes later, they were saying their "see you later's" as Carole planted herself in front of the TV, with Cecil at her side, for another reality network marathon. The three of them climbed into Tommy's BMW X4, and an hour after that—and against Tommy's strenuous objections—they were parking in the lot at the outlet mall. Tommy had envisioned a relaxing day at one of the local, upscale fashion malls. Saturday at the outlet mall was going to be hell.

"Do you understand how crowded it's going to be?" he implored. This was not what he was anticipating when Alex handed him the credit card.

But Ben was being pragmatic. He knew whatever they bought today would not fit Mike within a few of months. He didn't want to waste Alex's money and sacrifice their ROI.

"Listen, they've got Under Armour, Adidas, Nike, Polo, Banana Republic, J.Crew. We'll get in and out quickly."

First stop. Under Armour, where they got Mike his own compression shorts so that he didn't need to wear Tommy's for future photos. Between UA and Adidas, they got him two weeks' worth of workout clothes. Because of the stretch factor, these would have the best longevity. Even as they got tighter they'd only look better. Then they stopped at Polo, BR, and JC for shorts, jeans, slacks, polos and some casual shoes. Next, Calvin Klein for underwear, and Nike for athletic shoes and a gym bag. Ben and Tommy had fun playing dress-up with Mike as he tried on the outfits they were selecting for him. All three were loaded down with shopping bags as they walked toward the car.

"Wait a minute, I forgot something," said Ben.

"Something for me?" joked Tommy.

"No, we need to hit The North Face store."

There, Mike picked out shorts, shirts, trail shoes, and a backpack. "Now he's ready for outdoor weekend exercise. Let's head back into town. There are a couple more stops we need to make."

Tommy felt more at home in the parking lot of The Grove.

"Apple Store," Ben explained. There they bought a new MacBook Air. "He'll need this for school." And an iPhone. "This he just needs to live."

"One more stop, here. The Kiehl's store." Ben wanted Mike to start using high-quality moisturizers, sunscreens, shampoos, shaving creams, and deodorants. Despite his past, his skin was remarkably unflawed, and Ben saw a huge benefit in keeping it that way.

Tommy's car was jammed with their day's work.

Ben said, "No more shopping," and looking at his own iPhone, he told Tommy, "head to this address."

Tommy found a spot down the block from the Great Clips address Ben had given him. "What the fuck?"

"Hey, I don't want him looking too good before we start adding some muscle. This is a fitness makeover, not a beauty makeover. It's not about how good we can make this stud look with nice clothes and a good haircut, but how he looks climbing into *her*, or *his* bed."

Tommy had to admit, Ben had a plan. He was proud of his boyfriend.

They gave the stylist at the discount haircutter some basic direction. "Give Mike a trim and neaten him up."

"Shampoo?"

"Sure, give his scalp some loving."

When done, he was spun around in the chair.

"Looking good, Mike."

Mike ran his fingers through what was left of his dark hair. He had to admit, he looked and felt good. These guys were taking care of him. For the first time in a week, he wasn't feeling so overwhelmed.

Back at Carole's they unloaded all of Mike's new goods.

"Can you come by later?" asked Tommy.

"Let me see how Mike is doing. I'll text you in an hour."

"I miss having you to myself."

"Me too."

Standing next to Tommy's car, Ben grabbed the front of his shirt, pulled him close and kissed him. "Let me see what I can do."

When Ben got back into the house, the bags were still all stacked against the wall in their bedroom. Mike was lying on the bed booting up is MacBook.

"Say, Mike, would you be OK if I headed back with Tommy? Left you here alone for the night?"

"Hell, yeah. Go for it. I just want to play with my new computer, and research schools. I'll be OK. I'll text you if I need anything," he looked up holding his new phone.

"Thanks, man. I love the haircut," Ben said as he messed Mike's new do. "See you tomorrow."

"Have fun. Give Tommy my love, and thank him for today."

An hour later, Mike smelled popcorn. He headed to the living room to find the source. There was Carole, still sitting on the sofa, now wrapped in a blanket, holding a glass of wine, the big bowl of fluffy white kernels next to Cecil. The glow from the TV screen illuminated the wrinkles now lining her once stunning face.

"Grab a glass and come join me," she said.

The chardonnay was still cold as he filled his glass and sat down beside her.

"What's on?" he asked. Looking at the screen, he saw what looked like Ben's face. Younger and paler, but his eyes were unmistakable.

"Just getting caught up on our young friend's past," she said. And there was Ben, just as he'd described, being sold for an audience. "Child abuse takes many forms."

CHAPTER 28

Alex was a no-show for the second night, so Tommy and Ben watched *Mama Mia* on the big screen in the living room.

"I love Meryl," said Ben.

"Fuck that, Dominic Cooper is hot. Hell, I'd do Colin Firth."

"What's the deal with you and old guys? First Alex, now Colin Firth? And are the rumors of you and 'Mr. Top Gun' true?"

"Just my 'daddy complex' surfacing again. My therapist blamed it on a 'less than satisfactory father figure' in my formative years. But I think it's just too much drama with younger guys. Oh, and I never kiss and tell."

"Drama? I'll show you drama. Come to bed."

The TV was turned off and they disappeared into Tommy's bedroom. Maggie followed and lay down on the floor beside the bed.

Sunday, Ben picked up Mike from Carole's, Alex returned from the beach, and the four business partners/friends ate, drank, played, and partied around the pool.

Mike studied Ben and compared it to what he'd seen on the TV. His confidence in himself grew. If Ben could build a new life like this, then so could he.

Feeling happy from his weekend with Andre, Alex was the first to raise a glass in a toast. "First of all, Mike, nice trunks," he said, referring to the orange swimsuit from the outlet mall. "You too, Tommy. Thanks for wearing them. Guys, you're the best. I can't wait to see what this journey produces. I'm so happy to have all of you in my life, and I hope that you feel the same. Here's to our joint success!"

"Here's to *Project Mike!*" toasted Tommy.

Their enterprise now had a name.

They raised their glasses calling, "Project Mike," and sipped. Moments later, they were all jumping in the pool.

Later, while Alex was tending the steaks on the grill he called Mike over. "Still doing OK?" he asked.

"Yeah, really happy and motivated. Thanks for believing in me."

"Perfect. These are a lot of changes for you…happening fast…you let me know if anything is troubling you."

Mike nodded yes, smiled, and raised his glass before heading back toward the others.

CHAPTER 29

It was 6:00 a.m. Monday, and Sutton was back at the gym with her favorite trainer. She was well-rested since Franklin had spent the weekend in San Francisco with his kids. He'd explained to her that his ex had moved there after the divorce. He kept a place nearby so he could visit nearly every weekend. He'd begun to build a law practice up there as well. In her mind that was Franklin's first strike. She wasn't much of a fan of kids, nor the idea of being abandoned every weekend while he played daddy. He hadn't suggested that she meet them yet; it was too soon. But if they stayed together, that day would come. She shuddered thinking about it. Kids were like rich white guys, so "me, me, me." For her, there seemed to be no "mommy gene" and *never* "mom jeans."

"So what are we doing today, Benji?"

"We have a lot of time, so let's ease into it." She had scheduled a second hour to make up for missing her Friday session. Ben ran her through a warmup and some joint mobility exercises.

When that was done, he said, "Let's start with your lower body."

"I'd love to have you work on my lower body," she said in her sarcastic manner. Then she shook her head and said, "No, that was rude. I'm sorry. I'll be good."

"No worries." He led her over to the squat rack. After loading up the bar, he had her begin the movement. As she stared at herself in the mirror and moved up and down, she felt the strain in her glutes.

"That's good, Sutton. A little slower now. I have a question ..has your magazine ever done a makeover story?"

When she reached the top of the movement she took a breath and said, "Sure, that's kind of our bread and butter. We do them all the time. Gotta inspire the masses to get in shape to improve their look, health, and most importantly, their sex lives." She snickered.

She lowered herself into the next rep.

"Deeper," Ben urged.

Oh, the burn. And she was back up.

"One more."

Back down she went and when he nodded, slowly back up. He guided her back to the rack to rest the weight.

As he grabbed two five-pound plates to add to the bar he asked, "How do you select the stories?"

"What is this, Benji? Do you want to model for me in the magazine?" She wiped her neck with the towel.

"No, no, nothing like that. I was just curious. Next set."

Project Mike was too premature to discuss with Sutton. Hell, Mike hadn't even had his first workout with him yet. But he was hoping that knowing Sutton could provide him some valuable media channels to eventually pursue.

For the rest of their two hours together, Ben kept quiet about what he was working on. He put Sutton through a complete lower- and upper-body routine and let her talk about herself. She had done well in his eyes, and she was clearly exhausted.

"That's it for today. Make sure you drink lots of water. And don't just sit at your desk for the rest of the day. Walk around your office to keep the muscles loose and the blood flowing. And those heels you wear may make your legs and butt look good, but they aren't your friend. Kick them off whenever you can."

"Thanks, Benji, for noticing my ass. You know, if you have any story ideas you want to pitch to me, no promises that we'll use them, but I'll make the time to hear you out. Let's have lunch someday. And don't worry, I won't hit on you. I got me a hot black man with his own nice ass; I don't need your skinny white butt." She snapped her towel at him, winked, and strode away.

She might not know it, but he was already planning on taking her up on that offer one day soon.

CHAPTER 30

When Ben got back to Carole's, Mike was dressed in one of his new workout outfits. Ben had blocked out the afternoon to begin training Mike on nutrition and exercise. For now, they'd be reviewing things at the house and then heading to the gym to throw some weights around.

"What have you eaten today?"

"Carole gave me some Cheerios this morning. I haven't had anything for lunch yet."

It was nearly 1:00 p.m. *He must be starving,* thought Ben.

"OK, let's head toward the gym and get some lunch. We can review the nutrition plan there."

At the counter of the organic food deli, Ben asked Mike if he could order for him. He paid and they took their order number to a table by the window. Ben pulled out a spreadsheet, displayed as a calendar. Each day was spelled out with a choice of menu options and portion sizes, dictating the desired calories to be consumed. A few minutes later, their food was delivered to the table.

"Will there be anything else?" asked the pale girl with the heavy black eyeliner and nose ring.

"No, this should do it. Thanks," said Ben.

Mike looked at the basket in front him and laughing, asked, "What did you get me?"

"It's a simple turkey wrap. Some protein and vegetables. Nothing too heavy before a workout."

"It's green."

"That's a spinach tortilla. Low carb."

Mike bit into it. "Not bad." Then again, he was very hungry and this hadn't been fished from a garbage can.

The wrap was gone in ninety seconds and the chipotle slaw a few seconds after that.

Mike turned his attention to Ben's basket that hadn't been touched, "What did you get?"

"Spicy chicken wrap. Want to try it?"

Mike reached for it, then stopped. "Just kidding."

It was fun seeing Mike so relaxed and even playful. They'd come a long way in a week.

Some of the items on the spreadsheet were foreign to Mike, but he knew Ben would guide him through it. If the wrap he'd just consumed was any indication, then the food part of this was not going to be a hardship.

"What's this?" he asked pointing to the weekend section of the spreadsheet.

"Ah, beer," came the reply.

Mike was surprised.

"This is going to be a lot of work and require a great deal of discipline. But it's not prison. You need to be able to have some fun Especially when you start school. You'll make new friends, and want to go out for a beer after class on Friday or out on Saturday night. I could try to deny you altogether and have you cheat. I think it will work better if I just build it into the meal plan. Alex and Tommy are pretty healthy eaters, but they do like to drink. It's going to be damn hard living there if you feel like you can never join them."

Mike was committed to do whatever Ben asked, but he was relieved to hear that Ben was being practical in his approach. He hadn't had much opportunity to drink while he was homeless but in the last week he had already developed an appreciaton for it.

"I've got meals figured out for us as long as you're still at Carole's. Once you get settled in at Alex's, I'll show you how to shop for healthy groceries."

"Do you know when that will be?"

"No, I need to check with him. He did say this week though, so I'd plan for that."

Mike had grown very comfortable with Ben. He was going to miss being with him every night.

"Should we head to the gym and get started?"

"Let's do this."

"OK, let's go," said Ben as he clapped his hands in encouragement.

CHAPTER 31

"Everything in here needs to go," Alex said to the representative of the moving company who had come to give him a quote on clearing out the office and storing the contents

"Will you be packing or do you want me to quote that as well?"

"If you get me boxes, I can get it packed up." That was a good project for the guys.

"Very well. As far as storage, is it fine in our main warehouse with limited access or do you want a private storage unit that you can access at will?"

"Price it both ways." He didn't imagine needing immediate access to any of this, but if the price wasn't too much more, he'd go for it. He wasn't one to piss away money needlessly, but since the furniture belonged to his landlord, he figured it might be safer in isolation. And there may be some other junk he'd throw in there as he saw fit.

"I think I have everything I need. I'll e-mail you a quote by tomorrow morning," said the representative.

"And how quickly can you move it out of here?" Alex asked.

"If you accept the quote tomorrow, Tuesday, we could pick it up as early as Thursday morning."

"Perfect, that's what your ad said. I do love efficiency." Alex showed the man out.

Now he had to deal with furnishing the room for Mike. Renting was the only thing that made sense, given that this was just for twelve months. Alex was certain he could find what he needed online. He reclined on the sofa in the living room with his computer on his lap. Maggie climbed up next to him and rested her head on his leg.

"This beats dealing with traffic," he said to himself. "But Maggie, I can't see the screen." He gently pushed her head off to the side.

In less than an hour, he was done. He'd ordered a queen-size platform bed and a pillow-top mattress, matching side tables, a dresser, and lamps. It was a good-size room, so he also ordered a bookcase, a small desk, and a chair, assuming Mike would want to study in there. A few minutes later, a confirmation came through, guaranteeing that everything was in stock and scheduled for delivery on Thursday afternoon between 2:00 and 5:00 p.m.

Next, a quick visit to an online department store for fresh bed and bath linens. Select two-day, rush delivery for Thursday, and done. By the weekend, he'd have another roommate. What was he doing? But he remembered how lonely it had been back in that apartment in New York while first wife, Linda, had been on stage, and in his house back in Minnesota after David had left him. He loved having these guys around. They gave the place a spirit and energy.

Alex felt like having a cocktail—it was five o'clock after all, but decided to take Maggie for a walk first.

"Come on, Maggie; want to take me for a walk?" She jumped off the sofa as he got up himself. He slipped on the shoes he'd stashed by the door, snapped the leash onto Maggie's collar, and they were on their way.

They set out to walk the neighborhood at the foot of Runyon Canyon. A couple of blocks up the hill they came upon the dead end street at the entrance to the park. "It's been a while since we hiked up there," he said to Maggie. "Maybe later this week." The houses up here had similar views to his, he imagined, but the driveways were larger. The issue was the weekend traffic. Too many hikers hitting the canyon. It had to be annoying for anyone who lived this close.

"Hey, there's the black Aston Martin we saw driving down Sunset," he said to his canine companion, who was only focused on the squirrels in the trees. With its satin finish, it was one of a kind.

They turned and headed back down the hill. When they got to the house, Tommy's BMW was in the driveway.

"Tommy's home." Maggie's tail wagged. "Let's go say hi."

CHAPTER 32

By Wednesday, Mike was feeling the effects of his first two workouts. "I'm sore," he whined as he rolled over in bed. The workouts had been light so far. Ben had been focusing on getting Mike to master the form before advancing to much weight, but it was all new.

Ben chuckled. "That's to be expected. It's just soreness, though, right? No real pain. No injuries."

Mike shook his head.

"Where do you feel it?"

"Shoulders."

"Come here; sit on the edge of the bed."

Ben knelt behind him on the bed and massaged Mike's shoulders.

"Ahhh."

Mike knew he was going to miss this. He was moving into Alex's house on Friday. He was excited to have his own room, security, and relative privacy, even if he was going to have to share a bathroom with Tommy, but he had developed a genuine affection for Ben. He'd always liked girls, and had only been sexual with guys for survival. He didn't quite know what to make of the emotions he was feeling for Ben. He chalked it up to brotherly love. And that had him thinking about his own brother, wondering what had become of him.

After a few minutes, Ben said, "Listen, I've got to run. Wednesday means Sutton, first thing. Follow the menu for breakfast. and don't let Carole feed you any more processed cereal. I don't care what the box says about 'natural ingredients.' I'll pick you up for lunch and an afternoon workout."

There was a pause while Ben changed into his uniform. "Oh, and a long hot shower will help loosen you up. Fuck the drought. See you in a bit, bud."

Mike rolled onto his back with his MacBook. Time to do some more school research and Google whatever else came to mind.

CHAPTER 33

It had been a long week of learning how to shop for and prepare healthy food, and then there were the workout sessions, which had become more grueling as the week wore on. *It's going to be a long year,* flashed through Mike's mind.

Everyone was being very supportive, though. He'd even struck up conversations with a couple of regulars at the gym. He had to admit, he was feeling a kind of trust that had been foreign to him just a few weeks ago. And here he was, packing to move into Alex's house. Most of his things were still in the shopping bags from the store. Others were stacked neatly on the floor. His smelly, crusty workout clothes were cast into the corner in need of a wash.

As Mike stuffed the dirty clothes in his gym bag, Ben said, "I won't miss those stinking up my room. But on the flip side, they prove you've been working hard this week. Let's get everything loaded into my Jeep and head over to Alex's."

Rush hour traffic on Sunset slowed them down a bit, but a couple of hours later Mike was settled into his new room. He put new clothes into drawers and onto hangers in the closet. Alex had gone out of his way to make it feel like a dorm room with posters from the area colleges, UCLA and USC, hanging on the walls.

The four gathered for a dinner that Tommy had prepared. Healthy, of course. And no alcohol tonight—they were all going to start following Mike's diet by default, and they acknowledged that was probably a good thing.

"So, one last detail to attend to," said Alex. "What are we doing about a car for Magic Mike, here?" he asked, making a humorous reference to the movie featuring the hunky strippers.

Ben started to speak, but Tommy jumped in since researching the car had been his assignment. "We were thinking a Prius. Good economy, and it's a green option."

"Well, I was thinking a Z4," replied Alex, "but who cares what I think? And given what we've already got parked in the driveway, I'm not sure 'green' is necessarily what we're going for here. Has anyone asked Mike?"

It was at that moment Ben realized that he'd been "caretaking" Mike for the past two weeks. Maybe he'd needed to at first, but it was time for Mike to start standing on his own.

"Good point, Alex. Sorry, Mike, it's your car. What do you want to drive?"

Mike hesitated, not wanting to seem ungrateful. Stuttering at first, he said, "Well, I-I-I don't have a license to drive a car. I got a motorcycle license in high school when my friend, Dan, got his, but my parents wouldn't pay for the driver's ed classes."

"Do you want a motorcycle then?" asked Alex.

"I guess." replied Mike.

"Well, I've never bought one of those before. This is going to be fun. Do you know what kind you want? How about you guys?" Alex asked, looking at Ben and Tommy.

They shook their heads.

"Well, you better do your research tonight and figure it out," Alex told Mike. "We'll go motorcycle-shopping tomorrow."

Mike just smiled. He was excited inside but still wasn't comfortable showing it. He hadn't ridden for a long time.

They all slept under the same roof that night, and after breakfast Saturday morning, the four climbed in Alex's Range Rover to head to the motorcycle dealership the boys had found. Mike actually did have an idea of what he wanted. Dan and he had looked at motorcycle magazines in Dan's basement when Mike would hide out there from his family. He'd fantasized about getting a bike and riding away as fast as he could, but never saw a way that he could make it happen. Now it looked like he was getting the bike but no longer needed to run.

"Well, what do think?" asked Tommy.

The dealer had let Mike take the 600 CC Yamaha out for a quick spin. "It's really fun. I forgot how it feels.

The salesman approached, and Alex intercepted him calling back to the three, "You guys stay out of trouble. I'm going to talk to this nice man for a few minutes. "

Two minutes later an attendant came to retrieve the motorcycle from Mike. "This one's been sold. I need to get it cleaned up right away."

They weren't quite sure what had happened. Had someone else bought it?

Tommy knew Alex better than the rest and was fairly certain he understood what was going on. Mike was acting a little bummed, so Tommy directed the group to start looking at all the models around the showroom as a distraction.

Fifteen minutes later Alex came out carrying a thick envelope. He handed the keys to Mike.

"It's yours. These things scare me a lot. Promise me you'll always ride carefully, always wear a helmet, and for Christ's sake, no lane-splitting."

Mike could barely control himself. He hugged Alex as Tommy and Ben slapped him on the back in congratulations. More than ever, Mike felt committed and indebted to this group. They were quickly becoming his replacement family.

Alex then turned to Ben and Tommy, adding, "And next week, get him signed up for a driver's ed class. He lives in LA. He's going to need to drive a car someday."

CHAPTER 34

"Tomorrow marks three months," Ben said to Tommy and Mike over lunch one day.

"I know," Tommy replied. Looking at Mike, he said, "Time to take your progress pics and measurements."

"I'm ready and know the drill," Mike agreed. "After the workout, like last time?"

"Yeah, let's stay consistent," finished Ben.

The workout was taxing but doable. Afterward, Ben went back to work at the gym, and Mike took a shower at home. He checked himself in the mirror, pulled on his Under Armour compression shorts and joined Tommy in the garage where he'd again set up his once-a-month studio.

"Looking good," said Tommy. "Your muscle tone is really beginning to be defined." Of course, this wasn't new to Tommy. He was used to seeing Mike around the house and pool, wearing only shorts or swim trunks. Mike was looking particularly good today, though--he was still pumped from the workout. He'd been upgraded in his grooming to a full-service salon where he was getting regular, professional haircuts and grooming of his face, chest, leg, and arm hair. He had also begun to spray-tan, which complimented the natural sun he was getting between the pool and the regular trips to the beach and hiking with the guys.

This was now their fourth photography session, and Mike had memorized the poses. It could be drudgery, but Tommy kept it fun with jokes and rowdy music, and moved it along quickly.

"OK, time for the money shot."

Nice, the tan line was gone—the spray-on tan had evened it all out.

After a few poses, Tommy said, "Got it. Thanks, Mike. We'll show them to Ben when he comes by later."

Mike picked up his shorts and headed back to his room to read. He had an insatiable appetite for reading these days. He hadn't been able to start formal school yet. Even Tommy's impressive contacts couldn't get him into UCLA or USC. While he'd gotten good grades in high school, he hadn't tested well on his ACTs and had to settle for a community college, to start. He was hoping he'd be able to transfer at some point, in order to get a proper business education.

A few hours later, Mike heard Ben arrive and went to the living room to greet him.

"Is Alex around? I've got some news and he should hear it too."

"Did I hear my name?" Alex appeared from his wing of the house.

"Yeah, great. Come here."

Ben gestured to the large sofa and they all sat. He continued, "Tommy, how'd the shoot go today?"

"Great, I've got the photos ready to review right here." He held up his iPad.

"Perfect. I'm going to need them. I told you about Sutton. Well, during our session this morning, I pitched a quick overview of the program to her and asked if I could take her up on the lunch offer to review it. Her assistant called back this afternoon and confirmed a lunch for Friday. She's got all the media connections we could ask for to take this public in a big way."

Tommy was a bit shocked. He'd been around this town long enough to know how most of the offers people made were fake. He questioned whether she would come through for Ben.

Mike's reaction was more self-serving. He was suddenly a little self-conscious, thinking about his body suddenly being on public display.

Always supportive, Alex jumped in, congratulating Ben. "That's awesome, man. You persuaded me you could do this, and I'm witnessing the results. You've got this. I know you can get her on board, too."

Later, in bed, Tommy was reviewing the day's photos with Ben. Tommy had arranged them in a series, starting with the first shots of Mike fresh off the street.

"These are really good, Tommy."

"And the progress you're making with him is really impressive."

They shared a quick kiss then Ben continued to scroll.

"Wait. What are these?" he asked.

"Oh, you're not supposed to see those yet. It's something I've been working on for class."

Tommy had enrolled in a creative photography class at the local College of Art and Design. Since he'd picked up his camera three months ago, he'd been bitten by the photography bug.

Ben was now paging through a series of architectural shots Tommy had taken around town. There was nothing unique about the settings, but Ben was mesmerized by the use of lighting and shadows.

"Tommy, these are great."

"Thanks," he was uncharacteristically humbled.

"The lighting and shadowing is so stark. Even the daylight shots are spooky."

"I really liked that look. I'm thinking about trying to adapt that kind of look to the human form. I've seen it done with makeup before, but I want to try to achieve the look just through lighting."

"Do it. Spooky and sexy. Kind of like you," Ben chuckled, put the iPad aside and leaned in to hug Tommy. Sexy was just beginning.

CHAPTER 35

The satin-black Aston Martin was becoming a familiar sight in the circle drive outside the front door of Sutton's building. As was the handsome black man who often strolled through the lobby in the morning to retrieve it. The car was still there when she returned from her 6:00 a.m. training session with Ben. She'd left him to sleep in. Since he was still here, maybe they could have a little fun before work.

Franklin rolled over when she walked into the room. "Hey, babe," he mumbled.

She was energetic and came toward him, lifting the covers looking for some morning wood. And there it was. She was a bit sweaty from her workout, but as far as she was concerned, that was just the beginning. Sutton pulled off her clothes and stood naked in front of him. Ben had done a good job firming up the parts of her body that were threatening to sag from age. She was feeling good about how she looked.

"Come here, darlin'," he said with an uncharacteristic southern drawl.

He latched onto her hand and pulled her naked body onto his. She caught a glimpse of them in the mirror as they made love, and the song "Ebony and Ivory" flashed through her consciousness. *Damn, that's hot.* And she didn't even care for the song.

When they were done, she lay in Franklin's arms. Having the attention of Franklin made Sutton feel confident despite the uncertainty surrounding her job at the media empire she'd helped build. The latest insult from the man at the top was when he'd suggested last month that perhaps the "Letter from the Editor" would be better coming from the assistant editor, a former Olympic athlete and swimming star. She had to admit that the argument had some merit, given that it was a men's magazine and their demographic would probably prefer reading the insights of a male athlete rather than those of a female business whiz. Just the same, it was her decision to make and she wasn't going to let either of them bully her. Her numbers were strong and would stay that way under her leadership.

"I should probably get ready for work," she said reluctantly.

"How's your day look?" he asked, knowing her frustrations.

"Pretty light, actually. I promised to meet my trainer, Ben, for lunch, to hear him out on an idea he has for a body-and-lifestyle makeover." She paused, then resumed, "I've heard these before, so I'm not expecting too much. But he's a nice kid, and I thought I'd try to help him."

"Well, looking at your body, I'd say he knows what he's doing. Go again?"

"Damn, I can't. Join me in the shower?"

Forty minutes later they were riding down the elevator together. It stopped at the lobby, and he bent down to give her a deep kiss. She'd be continuing down to the parking garage.

"Have a great day, Sutton. Let me know how lunch goes."
Their hands lingered, intertwined for a few seconds, and then
he stepped away.

CHAPTER 36

It was 12:30 p.m., and Ben was waiting outside the restaurant for Sutton. He was ready. She'd tried quizzing him a bit during their session that morning, but he'd remained polite yet steadfast. He wanted his props with him before he let her in on what he was working on.

A Mercedes pulled up to valet stand. The attractive, blond Sutton reached for the young valet's hand as he helped her rise from her low-slung sports car. She spotted Ben and trotted over, her spiked heels clicking on the granite pavers. They were both surprised by their appearances—they had only ever seen each other in gym clothes. Sutton wore a bold, flowery dress and was looking quite sexy and feminine as the breeze made her skirt flutter. Once again, Ben commended himself for her shapely ass and legs. And maybe the heels were worth it.

"My, my Benji, don't you look handsome." Ben wore a fitted dark gray suit with a bright orange shirt that made his brown eyes pop. He was tan, his hair was combed, and his facial scruff was nicely trimmed. *Damn, even his shoes are polished,* Sutton noted.

They now regularly hugged after a session in the gym, but this was a business meeting, so he extended his hand to shake hers. It was a beautiful Southern California day, and they agreed to take a quiet table on the patio away from the street.

After they were seated, they exchanged small talk while they reviewed the pretentious menu options and placed their order with the waiter/likely actor wannabe.

"So, Benji, you've kept me in suspense too long. I'm a busy woman, how can I help you?"

"I really appreciate your time Sutton, and that you're taking this seriously. I've been working on a project for the last few months that is really starting to show results. I think the world would be interested in learning about it. I'm hoping you can help me take it public."

His delivery was a bit unpolished, but she was impressed anyway with his manner. "Tell me more."

Ben opened up the iPad and began a slide presentation. "I'm helping a young man turn his life around. He's twenty-two and until three months ago, he was homeless. With the help of an investor and a friend, we've gotten him off the streets, and I'm working on transforming his body through exercise and nutrition. He's a perfect case study on how, in a controlled environment, the body can be transformed."

"Sounds like a body-builder kind of story. Not very current."

"No, not a body builder. This is a lifestyle experiment." He began showing her pictures of Mike three months ago. "See here, he's a skinny, malnourished, scared kid. This isn't about adding a lot of mass. This is about letting his body develop into the form that's natural for him through a routine of exercise and good eating. It's all about being healthy, not looking a certain way. Watching his body and muscles naturally develop, and the confidence that comes from that." He advanced to pictures of Mike as of Wednesday with Tommy. But as you can see, he's developing into a very sexy young man. And it's because he looks natural, not like some muscle-head."

Sutton had to agree, this boy did look good. "And this is without makeup?"

"Just a spray tan, but no highlighting. He really looks like this. But there's more to the story."

"OK."

This isn't just exercise and nutrition. The young man has aspirations and is also now enrolled in college. He's a full-time student and fitting this in between his studies. Remember, three months ago he was a runaway, barely surviving on the street."

Sutton was interested. She didn't see quite yet how this was going to fit in with her magazine, but she thought it was a story that should be told. Luckily there were lots of ways to do that. But which would get the biggest audience and the biggest revenue stream? "So, I assume your goal with this is to make money. You say you have an investor—he or she must want their money back."

"Sure, we'd all like get rich off this, but I think we're all realistic, too. Right now, I'm most interested in making sure this guy has a chance for success in life," Ben pointed to a picture of Mike. "But if the story can help motivate others to live healthy, both in body and in mind, then let's capitalize on that."

"How many people are involved with this? How many mouths does this pie need to feed?"

Ben wasn't quite sure he understood the "pie" part of the question, but the first part was easy enough, "It's just my investor, Alex, who's is fronting the money and the housing, and my boyfriend who is taking the photos and providing moral support."

"Do you have a contract spelling out responsibilities and who gets how much of the pie?"

There was that *pie* reference again. "No."

"That could be a problem. How do you know this investor of yours?"

"He's my boyfriend's roommate and a good friend of ours. Kind of a father figure to us."

Friends and family often made the worst business partners. Sutton was now more skeptical of what she might be able to do here.

Then Ben offered up, "Would you like to meet him?"

What the hell, why not? thought Sutton. She liked Ben a lot and was curious about his boyfriend. And this investor sounded intriguing. She was a cynic. He was no doubt gay, probably preying on these young guys. She felt maternal all of a sudden. Where had that come from? And what about Mike? Cute kid. If nothing else, he might be a potential model for the magazine. But with everything going on at work, she was cautious about taking on a new venture—until she knew whether she'd be doing it with or without the magazine. "I'm interested Ben, but give me a few days to think about it."

"Sure thing, Sutton. Thanks for hearing me out," he said as their too-pretty-to-eat salads were served.

CHAPTER 37

Ben was back at the homeless youth program. He'd continued to come here most Sundays since bringing Mike home. He felt real pride, recognizing that what they were doing there provided hope for these kids. He felt they were making progress in their aim to keep them nourished and help them regain trust in adults. But he was disappointed that no one seemed to notice Mike was gone. The regulars were jaded by the kids that just stopped coming. In their eyes, Mike was just another one who had disappeared. If they only knew.

Occasionally an older homeless person would invade the group, usually looking to get their hands on something to sell for drugs or alcohol. In Ben's experience, they'd be rude but leave without incident. This week, though, the situation escalated While the kids were scattered around the facility for their music lessons, a man came in demanding money. The program administrator politely advised the man that he couldn't be there and needed to leave. An assistant offered brochures highlighting other programs for his age group. His temper rose quickly. A number of the volunteers circled as he pulled a knife. A 911 call was made while the man began swinging the knife wildly. One of the volunteers tried to grab his arm from behind. This distracted him enough that Ben could pounce. Soon the administrator and three of the volunteers had him pinned to the floor and pounded his hand against it until the knife fell free. The police came and quickly took control of the scene.

As they stood back up, one of the volunteers looked to Ben and said, "Are you OK?"

"Yeah I think so," Ben puts his hand to his cheek and when he pulled it away, there was blood.

"Here, sit down. Let's take a look at that."

The man had nicked Ben with the knife as he was swinging. And as they tackled him, Ben's head had collided with the man's. Ben's eye was beginning to swell.

"Get some ice," shouted the administrator to one of the volunteers. "And the first aid kit."

"Do you want to go to the hospital to get checked out?"

"No. I'll be fine. I feel fine. I'm sure it looks worse than it is."

Mike had wanted to come here with Ben. Ben assumed he felt he owed the program something, but Ben had put him off. Now he was certain he needed to protect Mike. Keep him away from here, at least for now.

Alex was playing the baby grand piano in the living room when Ben walked in. Ben had been around there a lot but had never seen or heard Alex play. He sounded amazing. These guys knew so little about Alex's past. To him it was ancient history. He loved to play, but they didn't need to know he had once performed with his first wife. Alex had a lot of rules for himself, and one was to not waste time reminiscing. In the rearview mirror things always shifted to the extremes— seeming much better or worse than they'd actually been. He continued to play a classical piece that Ben recognized but couldn't identify.

Alex looked up as Ben approached.

"What the fuck happened to you? Tommy, get out here."

Ben felt the bandage on his cheek, "Just a little fight at the volunteer gig. It's really not a big deal."

"Come over here. Let me see."

Alex had Ben sit next to him on the piano bench and lifted the edge of the Band-Aid.

Tommy walked in, "What's going on?"

"Our Ben here thinks he's a tough guy."

"Ouch."

"That's pretty deep. Did you have it looked at? You might need stitches."

"No, it never really bled much. One of the other volunteers is a nurse. She put some antiseptic on it and the bandage. Said to watch for infection. I'll be fine."

"And the black eye?" asked Tommy.

"Yeah, that's probably going to be ugly for a few days, but it adds character, don't you think?" Ben laughed. "Ouch."

As Alex reattached the bandage, Tommy said, "Probably going to leave a sexy scar," and he kissed the spot. "I don't want you going back there."

"We'll see. It wasn't the kids. But now I sure see another threat they face when they're not with us."

"How about a scotch?" suggested Alex.

"Sounds good. And something to eat?"

CHAPTER 38

Sutton left Franklin's house early Sunday morning and headed home to her condo. He had stayed in town this weekend and she had spent most of it with him. Between visiting the farmers' market, dinner, a trip to the mall, and a few other errands, she'd peppered him with legal questions, mainly about her contract with the magazine. He never claimed to be a contract expert and hadn't read hers specifically, but from a legal perspective, employment contracts were one of the simplest forms. Without providing much detail, she also waded into legal questions about Ben's proposal and how to go about instituting a contract when something was already in process. All his answers were qualified with the statement, "well that's not my area of expertise, but in my experience," or "I'd need more information to provide a realistic answer to that." His advice was helpful, but now her head was spinning with all sorts of ideas and additional questions for Ben and his partners.

"Where the hell you been?" The voice startled Sutton as she walked through her front door. "I was about the call the cops. Why haven't you been answering your phone?"

Wanda had come over, looking for Sutton, convinced something bad had happened to her dear friend and meal ticket.

"Battery went dead," Sutton replied placing a hand on her chest to calm her racing heart. "I spent the weekend with Franklin. It was nice not having this thing buzzing every five minutes." Sutton plugged it into the charging station. "Sorry I worried you. And thanks for caring."

"Someone's gotta look after you, silly white girl." They hugged.

"I've got to get cleaned up and to the airport. Help me pack?"

"Man, I do hate flying," said Wanda as she pulled out Sutton's roller bag. "Ain't sure what's worse, the tiny seats, rude stewardesses, or fear of dying in fiery crash."

"First class helps with the first two. As for the third, I'll just rely on alcohol and your prayers to get me through. I have to jump in the shower. Pack the normal conference wardrobe."

Then she was in a Town Car on her way to LAX. From there, she would be flying to Orlando for a media conference. The focus of the conference was on integrating print and electronic media, but she wasn't going there to learn. Sutton would be networking, just in case the wheels were in motion to dismiss her. Even if she wasn't being fired, maybe she'd get a better offer and could tell Malcolm to go fuck himself. She also saw it as an opportunity to test-market Ben's turnaround project—*Project Mike*.

When she landed, Sutton shot off a quick text message to Franklin, thanking him "for a lovely weekend" and for his "free advice." And then a text to Wanda, letting her know she'd landed safely.

The schedule included a cocktail reception Sunday evening. She had just enough time to check into her hotel, change into a sparkly black cocktail dress, red heels, and the two-carat diamond studs she'd bought herself after her second divorce. As she viewed herself in the mirror, she gave herself credit

138

for her ritual of 6:00 a.m. training sessions with Ben. She thought she looked at least five years younger than her contemporaries.

Sutton walked around the ballroom, reconnecting with a number of former colleagues and acquaintances. Without fail, each one commented on just how great she looked. Then it struck her—based on her own assessment and now the confirmation she was getting from those who had known her, some for many years—that Ben must know what he's doing. She'd been working with trainers since she'd turned thirty-five but had never experienced these results. She tried to think whether his routines were different. She certainly knew she was enjoying her sessions more than she had with other trainers. It's that magic combination of motivation, inspiration, and education. Ben was that good. She set out to work the room and identify who her best resources might be to bring *Project Mike* to market.

An hour later, she had a dozen business cards in hand, several coffee meetings set up for the next few days, and was headed back to her room. She pulled out her phone to text Ben to set up the meeting with the investor. On the screen, a missed text.

From Franklin: *We should talk.*

"Fuck," she said loud enough for anyone passing in the hallway to hear.

CHAPTER 39

Emmy parked her Prius in the driveway of Andre's beach house. She hadn't seen him in weeks and was anxious to catch up. Frankly, she was just plain horny, too.

"What's this?" asked Andre as he met her at the door. "Champagne? Veuve Clicquot, my favorite. Are we celebrating?"

"Just celebrating being together again. I've missed you."

"Aw," he said, and kissed her. He was used to kissing her while she was wearing heels, or when they were horizontal. In designer flip-flops, she was even shorter than he remembered, but the reach was worth the effort. He stood back up and took in the rest of the look. White short-shorts and the loose, pink silk tank top completed the beach-casual look. "You look amazing." He wrapped his arms around her and lifted her off the deck, kissing her properly. "Come on in, I made dinner."

Between his Mexican grandmother and his Italian mother, Andre had learned to cook both cuisines expertly. He frequently tried to blend the two. His meatball burrito was a big hit, but the spaghetti taco with hot sauce missed the mark. Tonight he'd stuck strictly to Italian, preparing angel-hair pasta with tomatoes in olive oil and a salad of leafy greens. He had a prosciutto-and-melon appetizer that would work beautifully with the champagne.

"Do you want to grab the glasses while I open this?" he asked Emmy.

"Sure." She stepped into the kitchen to retrieve the glasses and looked around. The place was spotless. Whenever she cooked, she made a mess. When Andre was on his game, he managed things meticulously.

Pop. He filled the two flutes.

"Salut." They sipped, and he kissed her again. He could taste the expensive champagne on her lips. He picked up a melon ball wrapped in ham and fed it to her with his fingers. The sweetness of the melon and saltiness of the cured ham played with her taste buds as she took another sip of wine.

Emmy stared into his gorgeous dark eyes and said, "How has some woman, *or guy*, not snatched you up for good?"

"Ah, I'm slippery, you see," he said with a mock Italian accent as he twirled around behind her and slid into the kitchen. He was being playful.

He returned a moment later, saying, "I just needed to check on the pasta," then sat down on the bar stool facing her. He picked up another wrapped melon ball and put it in his own mouth, chewed once or twice, then leaned forward to kiss her again. For a second her mind was thinking *this is gross*, but she was so caught up in the romance that she accepted the morsel into her own. Then she pulled his hand up to her lips and licked the salt from his fingertips with her tongue. They sipped again and she broke the trance.

"OK, mister, enough with the seduction. Let's eat dinner and catch up. I want to know what you've been doing for the last month."

He pouted briefly. He couldn't remember the last time his Italian Casanova routine had failed to lead him straight to the bed. But he was in a great mood, so he grabbed the salad and pasta and had her follow him to the table on the seaside deck.

For the next two hours they ate his tasty creation and talked about what he was dealing with. He was being run ragged, traveling from continent to continent, trying to save accounts while landing new ones. He had no time to be creative and design the buildings that were his passion. He was noticeably exhausted and thinner, but had spent the previous day at home alone, surfing and sleeping, which he swore had done him wonders. It was starting to get cool, and he suggested they light the fire pit and enjoy the rest of the evening cuddling and listening to the waves. She had another idea.

"Sit tight, while I clear these."

Andre was puzzled, but did as he was told. Emmy took the dishes into the kitchen. She returned to the deck a few minutes later having lost her shorts and bra, and was now wearing only her thong panties and the pink tank. Even in the dim light, her dark nipples were visible through the sheer fabric.

She picked up the champagne bottle and her glass saying, "Follow me," her round, naked ass bobbing lightly as she made her way to his bedroom.

The bulge in his tight pants made it difficult to walk. When he got to the bedroom, Emmy was lying on her back, propped up against the pillows, bottle in one hand, glass in the other. "Something to drink?"

Andre climbed on the bed straddling her. He took the bottle and glass from her hands and placed them on the side table. He kissed her and cupped her left breast with his right hand. After a minute, he rolled off her and stood up, first kicking off his leather driving shoes, then lifting his shirt over his head, exposing his trimmed but still thick, dark chest and stomach hair. He then unbuttoned his pants and pulled them down with his black briefs. He was fully erect and leaned forward to pull down her thong. A moment later his head was buried between her legs as she writhed in pleasure. Now her own hands were fondling her breasts through her silk top.

"I want you inside me," she cried.

He crawled up the bed until their mouths met again, and with her left hand she guided his member to its target.

Slowly he moved up and down her body. In then nearly back out.

"Faster," she moaned.

"No, just enjoy it, Em. I don't want this to end."

She grabbed his ass and nibbled his nipples as his chest heaved above her. Her own hips joined in to make his plunges feel even deeper. She came before he did and she trembled for what felt like minutes. His pace slowed again but, gently, he kept moving inside her. A few minutes later it was his turn.

"I'm coming," he moaned.

She wrapped her arm around his neck, and her legs came up around his thighs. She came again, just as he let loose inside her and onto the white linens. Her hands fell to her sides and grabbed at the sheets. He withdrew quickly. Both were sweating and breathing heavily. To herself she admitted that while the games and toys were fun, this night of traditional sex was the best they'd ever had together. And maybe the best sex she'd ever had, period. He collapsed next to her and suggested she lean over to turn off the light. A minute later, they were both sound asleep.

When Emmy woke up, the sun was breaking through the windows. Andre was seated at the edge of the bed with his back to her, still naked. She sat up, wearing her silk tank she'd fallen asleep in, and put her hand on his shoulder. He was shaking.

"Is everything all right?"

No response.

"Andre, you're worrying me, what's wrong?"

He slowly turned to her, he was crying.

"We lost our biggest project," and then he handed his phone to her where she saw a long message from his father, blaming Andre and calling him worthless and worse.

"Oh, Andy, I'm so sorry."

"Fuck, I don't know what to do anymore."

He stood up and walked to the bathroom and closed the door. Under different circumstances she would have made some sly compliment about his firm, hairy ass, but she stayed quiet. She could hear him peeing and then quiet. Then she heard him blowing his nose. A few minutes later he came out. He brushed his hand against her naked thigh.

"Hey, would you mind if I go surfing? I think it will help clear my head."

"No, that's a good idea. How long will you be gone? I'll make breakfast."

"About an hour, but don't bother with breakfast, when I get back I'll take you out. Let's spend the day together." He was suddenly sounding a lot more chipper.

"OK."

Andre walked naked through the living room to the back deck where his wetsuit was hanging next to his board. He knew the regular beachgoers this time of the morning were used to seeing him standing naked on his deck. A minute later, he was clad in black neoprene and heading down to the waves.

When Andre got back, Emmy was waiting, wearing a pale green sundress she'd retrieved from the back of her car.

"Gotta shower. I'll be ready in fifteen."

"No rush."

As he waited for the shower to warm up, he checked his face in the mirror. He noticed a little darkness under his eyes. Sure, he was feeling stressed, but he looked like he was holding up. What he didn't notice was the mirror that he'd left on the counter had been wiped clean and put away.

At brunch, she thought about what she had found in the bathroom. Clearly Andre was using drugs, coke specifically. Anything else, she wondered? Last night had been incredible, was that real or some drug-induced fling?

He hadn't noticed her somber mood right away, but when he did, said, "Hey, sorry about that this morning. I shouldn't have showed you the message from Papa. He was just blowing off some Mexican steam. I know how to handle him. I'm OK. Are you OK?"

"Yeah, sure. I was just thinking about something. I'm great, and happy to be here with you." She grabbed his hand and leaned in a bit to focus on him. Now her mind wandered to the sex they'd had. She chose to believe that it was genuine and the coke was just a pick-me-up he needed after the message from his father. Her mind still wandering, it landed on Andre and Alex, wondering what their sex was like. How did that work with the two of them? Oh, she'd seen gay porn, so she knew the ins and outs, so to speak. But who was the lead? Given how Andre sometimes let her tie him up, she imagined he might be the "bottom," but the idea of Andre lying there with his legs up in the air as his hairy ass got plumbed just didn't compute.

"After lunch, I was thinking we'd go for a drive up the coast."

"Sure, sounds great." Although the thought of being in his old convertible on PCH sounded windy and noisy, she was enjoying his company and committed to helping him relax.

North of Malibu, his phone vibrated on the center console and the screen lit up. He kept his eyes on the road while she glanced at it.

"You just got a text from Alex."

"Oh, yeah? What does it say?"

"Really, you want me to read it?" She was dying to.

"We've talked about the three of us getting together. I don't want to have secrets from you or him. So sure, go ahead."

"It says, 'Want to cum over tonight?' Come is spelled c-u-m."

Andre chuckled, "Yeah, that's him."

"So, are you going to drop me off and head over to hook up with him?"

"Jealous?"

"Should I be? Shouldn't I be? Yeah, I guess I am."

"Then come along."

She looked at him. He briefly diverted his eyes from the road and looked back. Then he laughed.

Emmy, reached over with her left hand and grabbed his crotch. "You're getting hard just thinking about it, aren't you?"

"Should I be? Shouldn't I be?"

She reached her hands up to her head to tuck her windswept hair back under the silk scarf she'd found in her purse. "I don't know, give me a minute to think about it."

He looked at her again, saying coyly, "I'll make sure you have fun."

She looked back at him then straight ahead.

Fifteen minutes later, as he was giving up on his charms, she whispered, "OK. But I'd better get plenty of attention. I don't want to be odd woman out."

Andre looked over at her in amazement, with his mouth open, and screamed, "Really?"

The quick turn had caused him to swerve the car slightly to the right and it caught the edge of the pavement until he could correct it.

"Watch it, cowboy, or we might not live to fulfill your fantasy."

In that moment, he realized she looked like a young Audrey Hepburn. Oh, her face was a bit rounder, but she had that effortless grace in her smile. Now he had to convince Alex.

But his confidence in his power of persuasion had just been boosted significantly.

"Text him back from my phone saying 'yes, and I'm bringing a friend,' he should be able to figure it out."

"Can I add a 'wink' emoji?"

"Not if we want him to believe it's coming from me."

She typed and confirmed, "Sent."

A few seconds later, "Emmy? What time?" appeared on the screen along with a happy face emoji. Maybe Andre was the top after all.

Back at the beach house, they both freshened up. After Andre spent an inordinate amount of time in the bathroom, Emmy went in to comb her hair. Once again, she found the mirror with white residue on the counter. When she came into the kitchen, she found Andre slamming a straight scotch.

"Another message from dear old Dad. He wants me on a plane to London tomorrow night." He poured another glass. Emmy tried to pull it away but he was too strong and managed to retain it spilling only a little on his shirt before draining the glass down his throat.

Emmy grabbed her purse off the counter saying huffily, "Come on, I'm driving!"

Andre was slurring his speech as he gave Emmy directions to Alex's "frat house," as he called it. The combination of coke and scotch was effectively dulling his brain.

"Just give me the address and I'll plug it into the GPS. Then shut the fuck up."

"Oh, don't be pissy. We're going to have fun tonight before I have to fly off and suck some client dick for Papa."

"Andre, please, just be quiet for a bit."

Andre barged into Alex's house with Emmy in tow. Alex rushed to meet them at the door. "Hi, Emmy, I'm Alex. Nice to meet you. I've heard a lot about you from Andre." He was lying to help her feel at ease. Andre had told him very little and suspected it was the same for her.

Emmy interrupted, "Hi, thanks. Listen, I had to drive tonight. He's pretty drunk, and I think he's stoned too. It's not good. I don't know how much he's told you. He's really struggling with his family."

Andre was weaving badly leaning on Emmy. Alex stepped in to help get him to the sofa.

"Well, Emmy, it's really nice to meet you, despite the circumstances. Yeah, I know a little about it, but I've never known him to try and cope this way."

"Obviously, nothing's going to happen tonight. I'm a little afraid of him right now. Afraid for him. He shouldn't be alone, so I hope you can take care of him."

Alex was impressed by the maturity of this young lady.

"Of course, Emmy."

As Alex and Emmy spoke, Andre managed to make his way to the bar and poured himself another scotch.

Just then Mike came from his room. In the three months, there had been a lot of physical gains. Honestly, it was time to go shopping again, based on how his clothes now hugged his expanding muscles. Mike took one look at Emmy and fumbled a "hi."

"Ah, it's the grand experiment, Project Mike, Michele, Miguel," bellowed Andre, speaking far too loud for the audience at hand.

Now Tommy and Ben entered the room to see what was happening. Alex and Emmy both noticed the fresh cocktail in his hand.

Andre continued, turning to Ben, "What is this, fucking Pygmalion? He's Eliza and you're Henry Higgins? Priceless, fucking priceless." Turning to Tommy, he said, "Just who's fucking who around here?"

"That's enough Andre," scolded Alex. He took the glass away from Andre and pushed him down hard onto the sofa.

"Listen, I'm going to leave," said Emmy. "It looks like you have plenty of muscle around here to handle him." She looked at Mike, Tommy, and Ben and then back at Alex, and said, "Nice meeting you." She made a quick exit.

"Prick," muttered Mike, fixed on Andre.

Andre was passed out on the sofa. Alex considered leaving him there, then said to the pack, "Come on, help me get him to bed. I want to know if he moves tonight."

They got him onto Alex's bed and stripped him to his underwear. Tommy had seen his body at the pool before, but Ben and Mike were newly impressed with Andre's physique.

"Thanks guys. We'll see what he has to say for himself in the morning," said Alex. "And, sorry, Mike and Ben—that was shitty thing for him to say. I don't think he meant it, but if he did, I'll take care of it. I promise."

"Oh, he meant it," growled Mike. Mike was clearly angry, a side of him they had never seen before.

"Come on, Mike," said Ben to diffuse the situation. Mike was still seething, hands clenched. "It's still early, let's all go for a swim and then a drink in the hot tub."

Turning to Alex, Ben said, "Thanks, Ax."

Mike and Ben headed to change into swim trunks. Tommy headed outside and dropped his shorts.

Andre's head was pounding the next morning. He didn't remember anything from the night before, but he was reasonably certain it hadn't been good. He knew he was in Alex's bed. He could hear Alex in the bathroom. Looking at his phone he could see he had a message from Emmy, so he was sure she wasn't around. He wasn't up to reading her text right now.

As Alex exited the bathroom and saw Andre sitting up, he said "Ah, Mr. Ocariz, how are you feeling this morning?"

Andre noticed how good Alex looked in his underwear. He was regretting whatever happened last night, because even if they had played, he didn't remember it. And that he would have wanted to remember.

"Fucked." replied Andre finally.

"Ha-ha, no I assure you that didn't happen. None of us had that pleasure. Emmy dropped you off and couldn't wait to get out of here."

"Argh." He rubbed his head.

"You're pretty fucked up, my friend. What's going on with you? I've shared a joint with you on occasion, but when did you start snorting coke?"

Busted. "Not now, Alex."

"OK, but you're not leaving this house until we have the conversation."

Alex lay back down and rolled over, knowing he had to be on an airplane in a few hours. He fell back asleep.
An hour later, Andre woke, smelling bacon coming from the kitchen. He walked out, wearing only his briefs, and found the source. At the gas cooktop, Alex was frying bacon and

scrambling eggs with Tommy, Ben, and Mike all sitting around the island.

"Ah, look who's up," said Alex. "Looking a little worse for wear, my friend."

True, but the other guys had to admit that despite the matted hair, Andre looked even sexier standing up. He may be an asshole, but they could see why Alex stuck with him.

"The boys and I thought a little grease would help get your head right. And block your arteries. After last night, win-win."

"OK, what happened? After the text from Emmy, it's clear I fucked up." Andre scarfed down the eggs and bacon, not concerned about the damage to his well-maintained body, while Alex replayed the events of the evening.

"Got it. I suck. Listen, I'm sorry." He wasn't convincing.

As he stood in the driveway waiting for the car service to pick him up, Andre said to Alex, "You're a fifty-year-old guy, with three twenty-something, male roommates. I'm sorry, but that's just weird. Grow up already."

Alex didn't bother correcting Andre on his age or that only two were actually roommates. He knew he had to be true to his word with the guys. Andre had to straighten up before he'd be allowed to come back here again.
"Take care of yourself, Andre. Be true to yourself and be happy. Let me know if I can help you clean up your act." He

kissed Andre's cheek and his hand lingered on Andre's shoulder as he got in the car. Andre just shook his head.

After the car pulled out of the driveway, Alex turned back to the house to see his three young friends watching. Together, they all went back into the house.

CHAPTER 40

Monday, 6:00 a.m. at the gym, Ben met Sutton for the first session since their lunch. In the last week, his cheek and eye had healed, so with any luck he wouldn't have to explain what had happened. "Good morning, Sutton. Ready to make up for lost time?"

"Ready. For the record, I did get in some good workouts at the conference. Better yet, I made some great contacts for your project."

"Does that mean it's now our project?"

"Let's not get ahead ourselves, but as I said in the text, I would like to meet your investor. We'll see where that leads. Have you set that up?"

"Yup, I talked with him about it. We're just waiting on your schedule."

"The sooner, the better."

"Ditto. Can you come to his house some evening for dinner? Might as well meet Mike, too."

"Perfect. You name the night."

"Tomorrow, then?"

"I'll be there. Now let's get to work—I'm feeling fat."

Ben intended the workout to be lighter, easing her back in after a week off, but Sutton hit it hard, asking him to up the load. She was having lunch with Franklin, and she was nervous about what he wanted to discuss. The exercise helped distract her and dissolve her anxiety.

By seven, she was sweaty and beat up, but she felt alive and wanted to maintain that feeling for the meeting with Franklin.

Shortly before nine, Sutton stepped off the elevator and through the glass doors of the magazine's offices. In the week that she'd been traveling, her new co-editor had moved into the large office next to hers, and the publisher had set up camp in the conference room, where she could now see him on the phone through the glass walls.

Lovely, she thought to herself. She had conceded on the co-editor, believing the male face was good for a magazine targeted to men. But what the hell was Malcolm doing here? Otherwise the office had the normal, lively buzz.

"Sutton, good to have you back," commented the publisher as he walked into her office unannounced.

Was that a jab at her for being gone for a week? "Malcolm, what an unexpected delight." Two could play that game.

"So what did you bring us back from Orlando? What's the latest scheme to make us rich?"

While he loved the money her multimedia empire made for him, he still didn't understand how digital made money. He was a traditionalist, preferring to deal in print.

"Oh, Malcolm, you're already rich. And you know I don't like to introduce things prematurely."

That had been an ongoing gripe of his, the length of time and investment required to bring any of her new ideas to market.

"That's what I'm worried about. Join me for lunch?"

"Sorry, I'm committed to lunch with a potential advertiser." She lied about the advertiser, but not about lunch. She had to meet Franklin.

"Maybe I should join you."

This was getting sticky. *Think fast.* "Certainly, we're going to the pier for sushi. Their choice." She knew he hated seafood and anything to do with the Pacific shore.

"Ah, maybe we can just catch up this afternoon then."

"Whatever you say, Captain," she loved facetiously stoking his massive ego. *Rich, white men*, she reminded herself, *always me, me, me.*

In truth, she was meeting Franklin at a bistro near her condo. He was already seated when she walked in.

He stood, grasped her hand and leaned forward to kiss her. She was suspicious, so she turned her head slightly, and his lips met her cheek. "Please, sit."

"What an unexpected surprise to see you in the daylight and in such a public place." She was being bitchy. They often got together in public during the day, at least on the weekends when he was in town.

"I take it you think you know why we're here," he said.

"My defenses are up, sure."

"I have a development…"

Suddenly she feared he was sick, or maybe dying.

He continued, "A couple of months ago, when I was in San Francisco for my oldest's birthday, my ex and I decided to take the kids out together. We all had a nice evening, and she and I ended up sleeping together."

Sutton was trying to process.

"As far as I was concerned, it was a one-time thing, and I was anxious to get back here to you."

So where was he going with this?

"I just found out she's pregnant."

WTF? He was a stickler about always using a condom with her, despite her proclamations of exclusivity and being on the pill.

"We've decided to reconcile and try to be a family again."

She sat there in silence. Multiple thoughts ran wild in her brain at the same time, clogging her synapses. Their divorce had been bitter. At least he hadn't slept with some random skank. Maybe that would have been better. No, they had a bond so maybe she should be less hurt it was with his ex. *WTF? How do I get out of here?*

"I don't know what I'm supposed to say. I'm happy for you? I hadn't even decided if I was in love with you or even starting to fall in love with you. You've never had a nice thing to say to me about her, and then you cheat on me with her."

They hadn't been served water yet, but she knew she wanted to, no *needed* to make a scene. This was Hollywood after all and her ire was rising rapidly. She picked up the glass of red wine that had just been served at the neighboring table, and threw it in his face making sure to stain his perfect white shirt and suit jacket in the process—if she wasn't going back to work today, then neither was he.

"Go fuck yourself, because you're never fucking me again." Turning to the next table she said, "He'll pay for that," indicating the wine. "In fact he'll pay for your whole lunch." She stormed out. She wanted to stop in the ladies room but feared if she didn't maintain her lead he might catch up to her. Her pride let her believe he was chasing after her. She headed straight to the valet stand maintaining her composure until her tires were out of the restaurant driveway. Now she was sobbing uncontrollably. She hit the speed dial for Parker who picked up on the first ring. "Can you come over to my place?"

"Sure, when?" asked Parker.

"NOW!" Sutton screamed.

"What's wrong?"

No reply. Sutton had disconnected.

It only took Sutton a few minutes to recompose herself. She could rationalize anything. A thousand reasons why this was a good thing flooded her brain. She called the office to say she wouldn't be coming back from lunch. Bad sushi was to blame.

Back at her condo, she looked at the gin, but opted instead for the champagne in the wine fridge. "Celebrate humiliation." By the time Parker arrived, half the bottle was gone. Together they commiserated. A second bottle was opened. Sutton swore the only thing she was going to miss was his chocolate skin and big black dick. Parker assured her those could both be easily replaced. By 5:00 p.m., they were curled up on Sutton's bed together, sleeping it off. Sutton loved her big sister and realized she could never move more than a few miles away from her. That would definitely limit her job prospects.

Parker left a few hours later. Sutton checked her e-mail, removed her makeup, put on her nightgown, and crawled under the covers. Today had been shitty. *Tomorrow will be much better*, she told herself.

CHAPTER 41

"What are you making for dinner?" Ben asked with a snicker as he entered the kitchen with Tommy.

Alex looked up from his tablet, "I don't know. I was just thinking about that. I thought maybe keep it very casual and grill some chicken or steaks. Or we could just order in— quasi-catered. Does she eat meat?"

"Oh, yeah. I told you she was a man eater. She eats men and cows. I think steaks would be great, plus Mike needs his protein."

"OK then, I'll head to the market in a bit. A salad and some vegetable for a side. A guy's meal."

CHAPTER 42

The phone rang in Sutton's car on her way to the office.

"How's your head this morning?" It was Parker.

"Actually, I feel really great. That's the most sleep I've gotten in months. Thanks for being there for me."

"I'll always be there for you, especially if it's to get over a man."

"Well, you won't have to worry about that for a while. I'm swearing off men. Time to focus on keeping my job and having fun with the project I told you about."

"Oh, honey, swear off men as boyfriends, not as boy-toys. Got to stay in practice."

"We'll see, Parker. Listen, I've got to run. Thanks for checking in, and thanks again for yesterday. Love you, sis. Bye."

"Bye back." But Sutton had already disconnected.

Malcolm looked up from the conference table as Sutton walked past and into her office.

"It's 8:30, what time does he get here?" she asked her assistant.

"He's been here since I came in at 8:00," was her reply. "He's probably still on New York time."

No sooner had she set her purse down on the desk than Malcolm came in and took a seat on her sofa.

"So, Sutton, are you feeling better? I told you sushi would get you. Did you at least close the deal before you lost your lunch?"

"Thanks for the concern, Malcolm. Yes, I'm feeling better. And yes, the sushi was the culprit. And yes, Bullhead Activewear will begin advertising across all our channels in three months." She had closed that deal two weeks ago.

"Why so long?"

"They want to launch with a whole new creative campaign."

"Oh."

"What do you want to talk about, Malcolm?" She decided being direct was the best approach with the old guy who controlled her fortunes.

"Well, I just want to make sure you're going to put Kyle next door to good use. We were quite lucky to get him fresh off of his Olympic performance. We're paying him quite a lot of money for his gold medals, and I don't want that squandered."

"Well, I…" Sutton tried to interrupt, but Malcolm kept talking.

"He's great-looking and charming, so get him naked"—he really meant shirtless—"in the magazine as much as you can.

I think he can write, too, so let him author the 'Letter from the Editor.' Someone else can write it if need be, but put his name on it."

"What about our digital media?" she had successfully cut him off.

"Ah, sure I guess."

"I mean, 'charming' and 'handsome' will come across much better in our podcasts and YouTube content, don't you think?"

"Whatever you think. I just don't want there to be any pettiness that gets in the way of capitalizing on the investment we've made here."

"Malcolm, you hurt me." She was livid but her demeanor did not show it. "You know I live for what's right for the magazine and its satellite channels. I'm excited to get to know Kyle and use him wherever we can to benefit all of us. I promise I'll make him feel very welcome and an important part of the team."

Sushi hadn't made her sick, but she thought she just might puke now from that spew of bullshit. Truth was Kyle was probably a nice guy, and there was no denying he was handsome, sexy, and by all accounts, smart. It was Malcolm she hated, and right now, she would say anything to get him out or her office…out of the building…out of town.

"Perfect. Thanks, dear." He put his hand on her shoulder. She hated that. "I'm headed back to New York in an hour."

Mission accomplished, thought both of them.

CHAPTER 43

"Ding, dong, dong, ding, dong, ding, ding, dong."

Alex hated that pretentious doorbell. Luckily, most everyone he knew in LA had free access to the house, so it rarely rang.

He heard Ben open the door and say, "Welcome, Sutton. Thanks for coming."

"Thanks for having me," came the reply. The voice sounded confident but pleasant.

Alex came around the corner from the kitchen as Ben was leading Sutton into the main living area. He reached out his hand, saying, "Hi, I'm Alex. It's very nice to meet you. Can I offer you a drink?"

She had not expected him to look like this. Very handsome. Forty-something, she guessed. Tall. Good physique. Another client of Ben's? Nicely dressed in tan linen slacks, a white button-up shirt with its long sleeves rolled up above the elbows, showing off some well-proportioned arms. His hair looked like a young Robert Redford's, and he had tender eyes and a beaming smile. *That smile must melt a lot of hearts,* she thought, nearly aloud.

"If you do, I'll accept." *What a stupid thing to say. A simple yes would have done.* She suddenly realized she was nervous. When did that happen?

"OK then, anything in particular? The bar is stocked. I've taught Tommy here to make a masterful martini."

Tommy entered from the guys' bedroom wing of the house.

Ben said, "This is my boyfriend, Tommy. He's our master photographer...and apparently our master martini maker."

"Hi, I'm Tommy. The boyfriend part is always up for review." They shook hands.

Tommy's diminutive height, shaggy blond hair, and squeaky voice reminded Sutton of a young boy. Oh, he was quite cute enough, but not what she had pictured for her handsome Ben.

"A martini sounds delightful, if you're up for making it, Tommy." *Delightful? Who the fuck says delightful? Did that sound demeaning? Maybe the martini will calm my nerves.*

"Who else wants a martini?"

"Sure, sounds good to me," said Alex.

"I'll stick with beer," said Ben.

"Come on in, Sutton," beckoned Alex.

"Lovely room. Have you lived here long?"

"Thanks. Not quite two years. I'm renting it, for the location and...view." They stepped onto the patio to see the same Santa Monica Mountains to the east she'd seen from Franklin's bedroom, what now seemed very long ago. The setting sun was reflecting orange off them, and the lights of Los Angeles were starting to illuminate the valley below.

"That's stunning," she said. *Good one Sutton. Very eloquent.*

Grasping for small talk, "I saw the piano inside, do you play or is it decoration like in so many Hollywood homes?" Franklin had one too, but it was dreadfully out of tune from lack of use.

"Oh, he plays," interjected Ben. "He's amazing."

"Yes, I play some," confirmed Alex. "It's an old story."

Tommy arrived with the martinis and a beer for Ben. He also had Mike with him and they each had a chardonnay.

"Sutton, this is Mike!"

"Hi," came from each of them in unison. They shook hands.

"This is the whole gang, Sutton. We're all glad you're here and want to be a part of this project we're all passionate about. Cheers to our success," toasted Alex.

"Cheers," came from all. They clinked their glasses and sipped.

"My, that is good," she said to Tommy.

"I told you he was good. I've got to get back in the kitchen," said Alex.

"Can I help with anything?" queried Sutton.

"The guys all have their jobs to do, so you could come and keep me company."

She followed closely behind with her stilettos clicking on the hardwood as she walked. Alex looked back at her feet. Sutton suddenly felt self-conscious, saying, "Sorry about the noise."

He laughed, "Don't be, it's just that we don't hear heels around here very often. Hell, we rarely wear shoes."

In the kitchen, Alex donned an apron. "I can make a mess of myself," he explained.

For the next twenty minutes, as he chopped and sliced salad ingredients and tossed them into a large bowl, he asked about her background and how she'd become involved in men's fitness. She told him. Her first job out of college was as an assistant to a family friend who started a chain of gyms. Soon she was writing the newsletter, then created the website. As the chain grew, a magazine was created and she led the effort. Eventually, the chain was sold to a competitor and the magazine was spun off to a bona fide publisher where it was retargeted specifically to men. For all intents and purposes, it was her baby.

Ben and Mike came in a few times to grab plates, glasses, and flatware to set the table on the patio. Sutton was impressed with the ease with which Alex navigated the kitchen and how well the crew seemed to work together.

They were all on their best behavior tonight. It was not unusual for the three of them to roughhouse around the pool, pushing one another in, pushing one another under in a feigned attempt at drowning, play keep-away. In so many ways, they behaved like brothers. But tonight they were all business.

"Tommy, is the grill ready?"

"Yessir, Master Alex," came the squeaky voice.

"Very funny. Come here and help me with the steaks."

"Oh, I've got it," said Sutton.

"Thanks, that would be great."

She had kicked off her noisy heels sitting at the counter, so she walked around to the other side in her bare feet, now stealthily quiet. She was beginning to relax around these guys, and around Alex specifically. She picked up the platter of seasoned steaks to take outside.

Over dinner, Sutton turned the tables on Alex. While she liked talking about herself and her successes, she was done answering questions about her qualifications. She wanted to know why she should partner up with him. He tried to get by only talking about his financial successes, but the guys prodded him about his personal life as well. They all knew some of the story but wanted to hear him tell it again. And Sutton was the perfect excuse. Maybe they'd get new details.

"I've read your Wikipedia page. Is it complete? There's little mention of a personal life."

"Tell her about your marriages," coaxed Tommy. "Those are suspiciously absent. We think he edited those out," he said, turning to her. "And your whole music career. It's like that was someone else."

"Oh, I don't think that's relevant to the topic at hand," protested Alex.

"Marriages?" asked Sutton. "More than one? And I assumed you must be gay like the rest of these guys?" She was known for being blunt, but even for her, this was out there. Rude even. Could she still blame nerves or was this some fumbled attempt at flirting?

"Hey, for the record, I'm not gay," chimed in Mike.

"Not yet, but we're working on him," joked Tommy.

Ben was worried this was descending somewhere it shouldn't go, but remained quiet.

"Ah well, yes, my sexuality has been somewhat, shall we say, fluid. But I was married to women, twice…a long time ago." Alex's calm tone, despite the sensitive topic, was putting her back at ease.

"And the music career? I thought you were a finance ace."

"Wife number one was a performer, and I helped her out a bit. I'm pretty good on the piano."

"Perhaps an after dinner, a concert is in order," suggested Sutton awkwardly.

"Yeah," cheered Tommy.

"Maybe some other time. Can we get back to the business at hand? You seem pretty engaged with our idea. Actually, Ben's idea, our project. Am I reading that right? Are you in?"

"Yes, I'm engaged and I'm in. This is going to be very successful, and I'm looking forward to getting a plan enacted," she said, trying to regain her professional composure.

A collective "Yay" came from the group.

"But, I understand that you're all pretty loosey-goosey on any sort of contract. We need to talk about that before I can get started."

"As far as I'm concerned, this is Ben's project. He created it and has done a good job executing so far. I'd like our roles to be as advisors to him and we'll have additional responsibilities to execute on."

Sutton nodded in agreement, "Makes sense."

Alex continued, "Ben, if it's OK with you, why don't Sutton and I take the lead on outlining contract terms and getting a lawyer to draft something that protects all our interests." He was looking at Ben. Turning his attention to Sutton, "She will also outline the marketing plan, responsibilities, and budget. Do you agree with that, Sutton?"

She liked the way he was taking control without being a bully about it. Might have to rethink her *rich white guy* theory. "Yes."

"Ben?"

"You know it. I couldn't have gotten it this far without you. Yes, and thanks so much," said Ben, relieved the pieces were finally coming together.

"Sutton, let's get together later this week, if you're available. We're obviously not ready to go to market yet, but it won't be long, and we should be prepared."

"Agreed, and I can make myself available. I do need to leave now, though, but how about a song before I go. She wanted to get out of there before she made any more stupid comments. But she wanted to hear him play, too. Help complete a little more of his picture.

Alex played *Piano Man*, and the three guys sang along. She was impressed with his touch on the keys, and seeing how all four of them interacted was truly delightful. That word was becoming part of her vocabulary after all. She laughed to herself. They had a unique bond that she didn't understand quite yet. She definitely needed to learn more. At least she had dismissed the idea of Alex as a predator.

After she left, the guys helped Alex clear the table, and they settled back out by the pool to discuss how they thought the dinner had gone and what they thought of Sutton. Alex was pacing on the pool deck as they talked. Tommy saw an opportunity, jumped up and pushed Alex, fully clothed into the pool. He was so distracted laughing that he didn't see Mike launching at him to follow suit. Tommy hit the water before he realized what was happening, and uncharacteristically, he was also still fully clothed. Then Ben pushed Mike and jumped in himself. Don Henley's *The Boys of Summer* was playing on the outdoor speakers, which seemed so appropriate at that moment. Maggie ran back and forth on the pool deck, barking at the spectacle. A soggy group hug followed before they each grabbed towels and ducked into their respective bedrooms.

"Are you staying over tonight?" asked Tommy.

"I should get back to Carole's. I haven't been there for a few nights, I've got Sutton at six a.m., and I don't have my work clothes with me. Can I borrow some gym shorts and a tee shirt for the drive home?"

"Sure thing. Help yourself."

"Goodnight, Mike," they called to his distant bedroom door.

"Night," came the reply.

Standing in the driveway, Tommy said, "You look good in my clothes."

"They're a little tight. Maybe I should have borrowed from Mike instead."

"No, everything is bulging in all the rights places." Tommy looked at Ben's arms, pecs, and on down. He kissed him goodnight, then watched Ben's Jeep head down the hill under the star-filled, LA night sky.

Chapter 44

"Come on Maggie, let's head up Runyon."

It was a warm LA day, and Alex needed some exercise and time to think. As he and Maggie headed up the steep trail, he stripped off his shirt to cool down and tan his muscular back and chest. Near the top, skin shiny with sweat, he stopped and took a seat on a large rock overlooking the city below.

"Here you go girl," he said to Maggie while pouring part of his water into her travel bowl. She lapped it up, then lay next to him in the shade of the rock while he sat and thought.

Alex wasn't sure what he was doing. Sutton had invited him away for the weekend, and he'd agreed. They'd been spending a great deal of time together, developing the plan to take *Project Mike* to market, and then just because they enjoyed each other's company. Over the six weeks since they'd met, their time together had become a cross between dating and acting like an old married couple—very intimate in many ways, but not affectionate. He hadn't expected or planned it to become romantic, which was clearly what it was beginning to look like.

It had been a long time since he'd been with a woman, though he was convinced both of his ex-wives would probably say he was pretty good at it. "Why am I hung up on that?" he asked himself out loud. Anyway, it took a while after those breakups, but he'd eventually turned his attention to men. He began to find their masculinity and physicality appealing. The firm embrace of a man was somehow very comforting. But repeatedly, he'd been hurt by them, too. The latest was

177

Andre, but there had been David before him, who had left so abruptly and without any explanation. At the end of the day, Alex wondered whether men, at least the ones he was attracted to, had the capacity or wherewithal to love him the way he knew he'd loved and been loved by his first wife, Linda.

He and Maggie stayed there for more than an hour before heading back down the hill. And now he was packing for a weekend in Palm Springs—*with a woman*, he reminded himself.

Tommy came into Alex's room, plopped down on the king-size bed next to the duffel bag, and leaned against the headboard. The gas fireplace was burning, despite the summer-like weather, to warm Alex after his shower. Dressed only in a fresh pair of shorts, Tommy noticed Alex appeared tan, fit, and…happy.

Tommy looked around the spacious room with its sparse collection of reminders from Alex's past. His eyes landed on the photo of him with Bruce Springsteen. Alex had told him how, many years ago, Linda, knowing Alex's preference for experiences over gifts, had arranged for him to play piano for a song with the E Street Band. They played *Jungleland*. Tommy wondered *how do you leave someone who can pull off something like that?* This river named Alex, or Ax, ran deep. His gaze moved to the view of the canyon through the massive glass wall, before settling back on Alex.

"Ah, lying here takes me back," he laughed.

"Don't get too comfortable, I don't want your brawny boyfriend beating me up."

Tommy sat up on the bed, wrapping his arms around his knees, and leaned toward Alex. "So what's going on here? What's the deal between you and Sutton? I thought it was a bad idea to mix business with pleasure. And since when do you like girls again?"

"Is that one question?"

"Yeah, but let me rephrase it for the slower members of our audience. What the hell are you doing, going away for a romantic weekend with your female business partner?"

"You told me I needed more friends my own age."

Tommy sprung forward in frustration. "Key word, Ax. *Friends*, not friend with benefits."

"I don't know. This just kind of happened."

"You're not rebounding after Andre, here, are you? And going straight because it's easier?" added Tommy. "Maybe a little nostalgic about Linda? I see you've got the photo of Bruce on the shelf."

"Well, I am kind of tired of getting my heart broken by guys. That hasn't happened with the women in my life."

"As I recall, you left both your wives. And why? To chase dick."

"No, that's not why I left them. Linda was my first, great love. But she and I just grew apart because she was so driven to work. Kind of ironic that she left show business and is a stay-at-home mom now." He sighed. "And Annie was a disaster from the beginning. She wasn't a bad person," he hastily added, though he knew he was being too polite, since Annie had been downright mean. "We just wanted different things in life. In reality, she was the 'rebound.' I think guys probably became my defense mechanism. And I thought I loved David as deeply as I loved, well anyone…until he fucked me over."

There was a long pause, but before Tommy could interject, Alex continued. "Listen, I don't know what, if anything, is going to happen with Sutton. I like her a lot. I think she's very attractive and one of the smartest and toughest women I've ever met. She's the first woman I've met since, well, since Linda, who understands my misguided logic and gives me feedback when it's offensive."

Tommy knew what he was saying. Alex's logic was rarely misguided, or offensive. But the list of things that got him worked up, simply because they were illogical, seemed endless. He had seen Sutton talk his older buddy down from those tirades as no one else could.

Alex continued, "And I think she really likes me for me. I just want to see how it plays out."

"I want you to be happy, Ax. You've been such a good friend. I'm here to support you as much as you've been there for me. I know Sutton is a good friend, too. I hate to see you fuck that up by, well, fucking. And I hate to see you leave our team. It's bad enough that we haven't been able to convert Mike to our debauchery. He's talking about girls like they're a good thing, too," Tommy laughed at his own misguided statement.

Alex ignored the comments about Mike, focusing on the sweet things he'd said before, and appreciating how profound his young friend was being. "Thanks Tommy. I love you, bud."

"Me too. Now let's rethink what you're packing, here. You're going to the desert, not church. Your old body has held up well. Don't you want to show it off?"

So, there was to be a fashion intervention after all. "Yeah well, thanks for the compliment, but this isn't a boys' pool-party weekend. The swim trunks and polos will be fine for the pool, and the linen shorts and oxfords for casual dinners and sightseeing."

"Suit yourself, Grandpa." Tommy got up to leave Alex to his packing. Before he left, he added, "Come spend the evening with us. Mike's here, Ben will be shortly. The four musketeers."

"Sounds great, but don't keep me up too late. I'm leaving early."

"It's a deal."

The guys spent the evening sprawled across the massive couch in the living room, watching Thursday Night Football.

"Why are we watching this," asked Tommy.

"Because some of us like sports," replied Ben.

"Are you sure you don't just like looking at the guys in their tight uniforms?"

Mike replied, "Not me." And he laughed. "But this sport is all about strategy. Sure, there's the physical piece, but there's time management and choosing the right play. Then there's the whole business side, spending big bucks on players, hoping they perform and don't get injured. Protecting your investment. Making lots of money."

They all looked at Mike, wondering where that speech had just come from. School was working for their newest friend.

"By the way," continued Mike. "I've been meaning to tell you guys." He was squirming a little with excitement. "I've got a date tomorrow."

"What?" cried Tommy.

"No way," said Ben.

"Tell us more," came from the always calm Alex.

"It's with Emmy Ayn."

"What? Alex's three-way?"

"Aborted three-way," corrected Alex.

"Yeah. As she was leaving that night, I said 'hi'. She seemed nice, so I tracked down her number and called her."

They were all in awe.

"Called? Nobody calls. A text, sure," said Tommy.

Ben remained silent, pondering what this might mean for his subject.

"That's what she said. I think she appreciated the effort. Is that OK, Ben?"

Alex began to speak, feeling the need to defend Mike, but Ben interrupted.

"Of course. It's great, in fact. God, I hope you don't feel like you can't have fun apart from us. All I ask is to be mindful of what you eat and drink. And get enough sleep. So where are you taking her?"

"Dinner, so we can talk. Then a walk."

"On the bike?" asked Tommy. "Or are you making her drive?"

"Of course not," said Alex. "Hey, Sutton is driving tomorrow, so take the Range Rover."

"Seriously?" asked Mike. He shouldn't have been surprised; Alex was always so generous. And he had made sure Mike had finally gotten his license.

"No problem. It's a fucking car."

"Enjoy your date, Mike. I need to go to bed now. Keep it down out here, OK?" chided Alex jokingly.

"PS, I Love You," Tommy said to Alex, referring to the Palm Springs slogan. "Have a great weekend. Full report when you're back."

Alex just waved him off, turned, and headed to bed.

"He's so great," said Ben. "How do we ever repay him for all he's done?"

"Let's start by making sure he gets his money back. Otherwise, just be here for him when he needs us. And given his history with relationships…" The statement from Tommy trailed off, needing no further explanation.

"Amen," said Mike. And they shared a three-way "high five" to seal the agreement.

CHAPTER 45

Alex dropped the Range Rover keys on the counter with a note saying, "Have fun!" Next, he was tucking his duffel into the tiny trunk of Sutton's Benz and climbing in for the two-hour drive to the desert. They'd be there in time for lunch and, as she suggested, some pool time after.

On the drive, they talked, laughed, and sang along to the radio, playing from one of his favorite iTunes playlists. He was surprised she knew all the words to *Born to Run*. At lunch, they ordered, then talked some more. As they were finishing, Alex placed his hand on Sutton's knee and ran it a few inches up her freshly waxed thigh. He had forgotten how the silky smooth flesh of woman felt. How it made him feel. Her legs opened slightly. She twitched and uttered a soft moan. He was committed. They never made it to the pool.

***

Back in LA, Mike completed his workout with Ben, and when he got home, asked Tommy to join him for a run. He had a lot of nervous energy and wanted to distract himself. It was a warm day as they ran shirtless down Sunset. Both received smiles and head-turns from girls and guys alike. Tommy noticed; Mike, not so much.

While Mike showered, Tommy took a look in the boy's now-crowded closet and made his selection for Mike to wear. A warm Friday evening. Southern California ease. Outdoor patio dining and a walk. His first choice was a light pair of khakis (linen pants were for old guys), and a dark-gray, silk polo shirt. Leather flip-flops for the feet, but he'd need to check Mike's toenails to make sure he was keeping up with his grooming.

"Is that it?" Mike asked as he came into the room, towel wrapped snuggly around his waist.

"Yeah, what do you think?"

"Hey, I'm not the fashionista. Everything about my appearance, from my wardrobe to my body, even my hair and beard, are thanks to you and Ben. I'm not going to weigh in now. But, yeah, it looks great."

Tommy had forgotten to check the toenails, but when Mike dropped the towel to pull on his underwear, Tommy could tell from the fresh grooming around the groin that the toenails were no doubt fine.

Dressed, Mike posed for Tommy. The clothes fit his body nicely. The khakis hugged his now-rounded ass, and the polo stretched across his shoulders and pecs, then hung loosely against his flat belly. Mike's hair was finger combed, with just a small amount of hair product, into an effortless style.

"Let me grab my camera. Alex and Ben are going to want to see this."

Mike checked the clock on his phone as he approached the block with Emmy's apartment. He was a few minutes early, so he circled again. Inside, he was greeted by a concierge who relayed that Emmy would be down shortly. Ten minutes of pacing later, the elevator chimed and Emmy came bouncing out. His heart soared. She looked beautiful. Much more like a young girl going on a date rather than the successful model he'd studied up on, online. She wore an indigo-blue, lightweight, sleeveless cotton dress. Though she was covered up on top, he could see a long slit down the middle, and her breasts were moving freely inside. The skirt was quite short, showing off her thin but shapely legs. She had only the lightest of makeup on her face, allowing her flawless dark skin and natural beauty show through. All of this was topped with long, silky black hair that hung softly around her face. Man, he felt out of his league. How had he gotten here? A quick hug later, they were in Alex's Range Rover and on their way to the restaurant, valet parking, and their patio table with a view of the orange and pink sunset on the darkening waves.

Up to this point it had been small talk, but the moment their cocktails arrived, Emmy began the inquisition. She had a million questions, and once Mike figured out what was going on, he committed to answering them honestly. He liked this girl but knew he had to be himself. She'd either like him or not. The way he had been accepted, despite his past, by Alex, Tommy and Ben, gave him confidence.

"So, where are you from?"

"Portland, originally. But I haven't been back there for a while."

"Is your family still there?"

"As far as I know. I haven't talked to them since I left. Listen Emmy, my story is complicated. If you're interested, I'll tell you everything. But I don't want tell it piecemeal, question by question, or bore you with an extended tale of woe, either."

She sipped her drink, sat back with her arms folded across her chest, and said, "Hit me."

Mike was momentarily distracted by how her pose caused her dress to open slightly, exposing the round curves of her breasts.

Regaining his composure and shifting his eyes back up to meet hers, Mike spilled his guts. Trying not to sound whiny, he told her of being sexually abused by his stepfather. He told her his biological father was in prison, and his stepfather was a crook and should be. He had an older brother who had run away years before and was probably dead. He told her of his difficult relationship with his mother after her defense of her husband. He told her of running away himself and living on the streets. He told her of turning tricks with "dirty old men" to get money. He told her of the stabbings.

She was stunned. Didn't quite know what to say, but managed to lean forward and reach for his hand, "I'm so sorry. So, Ben found you and helped you make a new life."

"Yes, Ben found me, but I'd have to credit Alex for giving me a new life. He's paying for all this. And it was really my friend Holly who pushed me. She's someone I met when I first got to LA. She's pretty messed up, on drugs. She kept me from going that direction. She made me promise to find a way out."

"Have you seen her? Does she know what's happened to you?"

"I can't find her. I've driven around. Her phone isn't working And I can't think of anyone who would know her. I'm afraid for her. Afraid she might be gone…dead."

Emmy realized she was grasping his hand perhaps too tightly. His story was so different than her own that it was hard to comprehend. She knew it had to have been hell. How do people survive that? Find hope?

"So, enough about me and my sob story, tell me about your fabulous life," Mike said, trying to lighten the mood.

"Not so fast, I have a question. Are you alright? I mean, really, there must be some PTSD or something associated with this. Are you seeing anyone who can help you through this? Someone to talk to?"

"Ah, you mean like, am I crazy?" He rolled his eyes around in his head and waved his fingers.

"No, I don't mean it like you're dangerous or that I'm afraid of you. It just seems like all this change can be a great distraction, but that could mean you're just repressing feelings that will surface later."

"Are you a shrink, pretty lady? You may have missed your calling."

She was feeling a bit exasperated. He didn't seem to be listening to her. "I'm just saying, I've been through some shit myself, and I know it helped me to be able to talk about it."

"Sorry. Yeah, actually Alex hooked me up with a psychiatrist who I've seen a few times. She's been really great. She knows Alex, and has met Ben and Tommy and says they're a great support group for me. They know the whole story, so I don't have to keep anything secret from them."

"This Alex guy seems to have it all together. Maybe I should have stuck around that night. Could have been fun." Emmy was being facetious, but Alex did sound too good to be true.

"I owe everything to Alex. I trust him like I've never been able to trust anyone else who is older. And Tommy and Ben are like the best brothers I can imagine."

She clasped his hand harder, "Thanks for being so open with me. It's amazing how well you're coping with everything."

"Back to you." He tried again, desperately, to change the subject. This wasn't going to be a pity party. "So, let's hear about your skeletons."

Her background was much more solid. She had some issues growing up half Asian, half black—she was an outsider, not fitting into either group. Her parents had pushed her hard, and she had excelled academically, which had led to an eating disorder. That's when she had visited with mental health professionals. She'd fallen into the modeling gig and was banking as much money as she could.

"So, we're both pretty fucked up. Want another drink?"

She laughed and said, "Sure."

They had another cocktail, ordered dinner, and then took a long walk. By now the conversation had turned to the future—their dreams and goals.

"It's so great that we can talk about our future so optimistically. I don't know about you, but there was definitely a time when I didn't want to go on. But now I want to take the money I'm making modeling and start my own company."

"I can relate. That's why I'm taking business classes," said Mike. He was holding her hand as they walked, and he could feel the warm blood pumping in their clasp.

"New topic. So, what were you doing with that asshole Andre?" He really didn't understand Andre's appeal, to Alex or to Emmy.

"Ha-ha, you mean other than he's gorgeous?"

"Not my type."

"Well if you were into that kind of thing, he has an enormous penis. Ask Alex."

"Fair enough, but come on, the guy's a jerk."

"He wasn't like that when I first met him. He was fun and energetic, and adventurous. He liked to be active and have a good time. He made me laugh. And seriously, he can be very sweet in bed. The last few months, though, he's been under a lot of pressure from his father. He's worked hard for the company and gotten lots of new clients on his own and designed some beautiful buildings, but his dad always wants more from him, to make up for his brother's shortcomings. I think he's just cracking under the pressure. I feel bad for him."

"So, he's handsome with a big dick, strike one. Good in bed, strike two. What else don't I have? Let's go for a strikeout. Oh wait, he's rich, too. I guess I'm tagged before making it to first."

She bumped her shoulder into his, throwing him off balance as they walked. "Hey, I'm here with you, aren't I? And for the record, you are kind of cute."

"Ouch, *cute*." He mimicked a knife stabbing his heart. The unconscious gesture gave him a momentary, painful flashback, but he quickly refocused on her.

"Hey, don't underestimate cute."

He stopped and turned to face her, bent down, and gently kissed her luscious lips. She responded, and his hand wrapped around the back of her head to pull her in even closer. Her hair was so soft. He lost track of how long they held that pose. When it ended, his heart was racing.

They walked back to his car, and he drove to her place. At the front door, he kissed her again. Her hand caressed his neatly trimmed beard. It was so soft to touch.

"I'd ask you in, but I think we both need a little time to process. I like you a lot, and I don't want to rush this. We both could be a little vulnerable right now."

"I understand, doctor. But tell me you'll see me again."

"That I can promise. Call me tomorrow."

Another kiss. He waited for her to get safely inside before turning back for the drive home.

CHAPTER 46

After the weekend in Palm Springs, the relationship between
Alex and Sutton continued to grow. What had started as a
business arrangement and evolved into friendship was now a
full-fledged love affair. They spent as much time together as
they could. Only work and its respective travel kept her from
him.

Alex was spending most of his nights at Sutton's condo these
days. He knew it was easier for her. And he had to admit that
he enjoyed being able to walk to the Starbuck's on the corner
before jumping in his Range Rover for the drive back to his
place in the Hollywood hills.

Sutton had already left for the office when, coming out of the
shower, Alex ran into Wanda. He didn't notice her in the
bedroom doorway at first, as he stood there drying himself
with the thick terry towel.

"My, my, you must be the new Mr. Man," he heard come
across the vast room. "She didn't tell me you'd be here…in
all your glory."

Alex quickly wrapped the towel around his waist to conceal
his junk. "Sorry about that, you must be Wanda. I've heard a
lot about you." Alex crossed with his right hand extended and
his left firmly holding the towel in place. "She didn't tell me
you'd be here, either, and she talks about you a lot. Sutton
thinks the world of you. It's nice to finally meet you. Sorry
again about flashing you. I'll just get dressed and get out of
your way."

"No hurry, I'm enjoying the view." Wanda cackled. "You're even handsomer than the picture she showed me. Of course the picture had clothes on. Didn't do you justice." Still cackling.

Regaining her composure, she said, "I'll leave you alone to get your pants on. Say goodbye before you leave, so I know when it's safe to come in here to straighten up. Them sheets probably need changing," she snorted as she turned and left.

Later that evening Alex and Sutton were lying together in her bed. Fresh white sheets smelled vaguely like lavender.

"So, I met Wanda this morning."

Sutton chuckled softly, "So I heard. Gave her quite an eyeful, she said."

"Yeah, I've become an exhibitionist, like Tommy."

"That works for me," she replied as she rolled onto her side, put her hand on his bare chest, and leaned in to kiss his lips. Her hand stroked the chest hair that he was no longer shaving. A bit of gray was now visible against his dark tan. Since he began dating Sutton, he was becoming less obsessed with trying to look as youthful as possible. She was helping to make him appreciate the value of his years.

"How is Tommy doing? I see Ben and Mike at the gym, but with you coming over here, I don't ever get to see him."

"He's doing well. I'm not seeing him as much, either. He's reconnected with his parents a bit and spending more of his days in Beverly Hills. He's even doing some photography work for them. It's great that he's rediscovered his love for taking pictures."

"You are such a good influence on those kids. I understand how you all met, but why did you take on this role with them?"

"What role?"

"Well, I'd have to call it, ah, their protector."

"Oh, I don't think of it like that. In fact, I think I'm pretty selfish about it. There's a lot more in it for me than them."

Sutton looked at him with a puzzled expression.

"I've never been very fond of self-centered people. And most people are that way. That's one reason I don't have many close friends."

"But," she tried to interrupt with a question. Alex cut her off.

"Let me finish this stream of consciousness before I lose it. Most guys, and a lot of women, too, once they hit their stride in their careers, are so worried about protecting everything they've gained that they become 'me, me, me'-focused. Oh, they can be friendly enough, but at the end of the day, any activity, any conversation can't be just fun, it has to mean something for them. It's all about 'what's in it for me.' Very young kids are the same way but for different reasons. That may be why I never wanted babies. But they're learning, and so I can kind of excuse it with them."

As he talked, Sutton's mind went to Malcolm, a perfect example of a rich white guy trying to protect what he had. And the comment about kids. Maybe that behavior had influenced her own view on kids. Everything Alex was saying was making so much sense to her.

He continued, "But with these young guys, they're different. Because they don't have much yet, they aren't afraid of losing it. They're just much more open…to everything…and everyone. I guess they're kind of naive. That's refreshing to me. And maybe down deep, I want to nurture that somehow."

"I get it, what you're saying. I haven't spent a lot of time around that age group. By the time they get to me at the magazine, they've already got their goals mapped out and are hell-bent on making their mark." She was now absentmindedly playing with the gold locket she was wearing. She let go of it, and it fell back to her chest as she again reached out to touch his. "So, why don't you ever talk about your past?"

"What are you talking about? You know plenty about me."

"Only what I've been able to read online. Or what the guys have been able to find out and have told me. I want to hear it from you."

"I guess I don't talk about it because now, it all seems so surreal. It's like it happened a thousand years ago. And it's so far removed from where I am today. It was all, well mostly, great. But I can't repeat it. It just happened. None of it was planned. And I don't want to repeat it. Dwelling on it just distracts me from the present."

"But everything you've done, accomplished, lived through, helped shape who you are. And that guy's pretty wonderful."

"Like I said, I want to focus on now."

She thought he might be getting a little annoyed with her, but then he asked, "Want to fuck?"

"Yes," came her relieved reply.

He leaned over to kiss her.

She pushed him back, "But not until you tell me something I don't already know about you."

"OK." He paused for a moment. "I lost my virginity to my first wife on our first date. I was twenty. She initiated it. I think I equated the feeling of orgasm to love. So I married her."

"But you've told me you did love her."

"Oh, I did. But it took me a while to figure out that the ecstasy of sex isn't love. I always liked her, and we genuinely fell in love over time. But I think a lot of people get confused on this, equating sex with love."

"Yeah, I get that," thinking now about Franklin and hoping she wasn't making the same mistake with Alex. Their sex was good, really good. Then moving the conversation along, "So why did you wait until you were twenty? Rich. Handsome. You must have had lots of girls...and guys pursuing you."

"Not really. I think I projected a confidence that put people off. And my network was a lot of shallow, rich kids. But really, I was pretty shy."

There was a long pause. Sutton was once again playing with her locket. Finally, she asked what she had wanted to for some time. "So, how did you make the leap to guys after that?"

"Oh, that took a while…and a couple more failed relationships with women." Alex turned toward Sutton with a quizzical look, "Do you really want to talk about this?"

"It's part of your story. Of course I do. I'm in love with you." There it was. It was out there. She had said the "L" word.

He was staring at the ceiling now, reflecting.

"It was with my mom's boyfriend. Oh, he was a lot younger than her. After my dad died she turned into a real cougar." Alex laughed. "He was only a few years older than me. We always got along well. When they broke up, he decided to move to San Diego. I offered to help, and we did a road trip out there. We were driving for five days and having a great time. The night before we got to San Diego, we stayed at a motel in Sedona. It wasn't that I suddenly realized I was attracted to him, I just felt really close to him right then, and expressing that physically just seemed right. Maybe it was the vortexes." He laughed again, and his hand was twirling in the space above his face. "We drank too many beers and ended up making out. I gave my first blow job. That was it. No regrets from either of us. He still lives in San Diego. Sweet wife, two great kids."

"So, you stay in touch with him?"

"It's been a while, but I consider him to be a good friend and confidant. We talk on the phone and make a point to grab a beer when he gets up to LA. I'd like you to meet him."

Sutton smiled and grabbed his arm.

"Well, that sounds pretty innocent, in the scheme of things," she said.

"I guess. But it lowered both of our inhibitions. He dabbled with the same-sex lifestyle for a while until he met Amy. I didn't date anybody for a long time, but when I met David, I fell hard. He had a complicated story, and we moved in together pretty fast, so it's not surprising that it blew up the way it did. It was painful though, and I don't talk about it much."

"Anyone after David?"

"Well, Tommy briefly, as you know. And then Andre. But Tommy was always more of a friend, and Andre was intense but never serious."

Her hand was mindlessly playing with the hair on his arm that was now back on his own chest.

He turned back to her. "There, was that the price of admission?"

"Nice choice of words. Come here." And she pulled him on top of her. She'd have to remember this tactic to get him to open up more.

CHAPTER 47

Given Sutton's work and, now, her social calendar, even Parker found it hard to schedule time with her. But her persistence finally got her an invitation to join Sutton for dinner at Alex's house. Alex and Sutton's worlds were really starting to blend.

"I do want you to meet Alex," Sutton confirmed to Parker, "and the whole gang."

Ding, dong, dong, ding, dong, ding, ding, dong.

Hearing the Westminster chime reminded Parker of her own back in Brentwood. She felt rather comforted by it. In addition to loving Sutton, she also had this in common with Alex.

Alex joined Sutton at the door to greet Parker.

After Sutton hugged Parker, Alex reached his hand forward saying, "Hi Parker, it's so nice to meet you. I'm Alex."

"It's nice to meet you too, Alex. I've heard a ton about you from our girl here."

"As I have about you. Sutton, why don't you show Parker into the living room and set her up with a drink while I go get the guys."

Sutton nodded and winked at Alex, and took Parker's hand.

"My, he is quite handsome, isn't he? Almost as hot as Franklin. But the white boy's probably not hung as well. Pity."

"Don't worry about that. He stacks up nicely. Not that I compare those types of things."

They both laughed as Sutton poured them each a glass of wine.

"So, this is quite a nice place," noticed Parker.

"Come out here and look at the view."

As they were looking at the lights of the city below, Alex came outside with Tommy and Ben. Mike trailing behind, as always.

"Parker, I'd like you to meet my friends, Tommy, Ben, and Mike," introduced Alex.

They each shook her hand and collectively began to size her up. She was every bit as attractive as Sutton. Very well-maintained. If they hadn't been told, they would not have known she was the elder sister by three years. And while Sutton had now adopted a more easy-going appearance around the guys—less makeup, softer hair, casual dress— Parker looked as though she was always ready for an audience with someone important. They already knew they wanted to see her Brentwood estate, to complete the picture. They'd search for photos online, later.

"My, they're all quite handsome and fit. Which one is the 'project'?" asked Parker.

Tommy spoke up, "Mike here is Pygmalion." They'd all started joking about that since Andre's harsh remarks. "Ben is Henry Higgins, and I'm just the voyeur—I take the pictures to document it."

"Tommy's selling himself short," said Mike. "He's a tremendous coach. He gets me up and out to the gym when I don't want to go, watches what I eat, and even trains with me sometimes."

Ben added, "He's really good at the photography piece too."

"He is," confirmed Alex.

"I'd love to see your photography. Would you show me?"

Tommy eagerly agreed.

"Guys, come help me with dinner. We're serving the ladies tonight."

"Thanks, Ax." Sutton loved using the nickname the guys had coined for Alex. She again took Parker's hand and led her to the seating area at the edge of the patio, where they could talk and enjoy the view.

"Well?"

"I must say, they're a handsome lot. And very polite. I don't really get it, though. Feels like the early stages of a cult. The dynamic leader and his eager, young followers."

"Parker, don't be like that."

"Oh, you know me. I'm just being catty. But it is awfully soon after Franklin and—"

"I was never in love with Franklin," Sutton interrupted.

"So you're in love with Jim Jones, here?"

Sutton looked into Parker's eyes and whispered, "Yes...I think I am."

Mike interrupted to offer a refill on their wine.

"Thanks, Mike."

After he left, Parker continued. "Sutton, I don't want to see you get hurt. He's bi, right? Are you sure he wants a woman? I mean, he lives with three cute, young guys. Something has to be up with that. And I'm guessing they don't pay rent."

"My, you are being catty. Really bitchy, actually." This wasn't the time to explain what Alex had told her. And she may never confess that to Parker.

"I'm sorry, Sutton. I don't know what I'm talking about. He seems lovely, and I look forward to getting to know him better. Your big sister is just being protective."

"That's the Parker I love." She put her head on Parker's shoulder and clinked glasses.

"Ladies," came a gentle voice from right behind them. "Would you join us for dinner?"

Parker looked at Sutton, wondering how much Alex had just heard. They stood up.

"You too, Maggie." She had joined the ladies, lying on the flagstone between their feet, for the "girl talk."

As they turned around, they saw Tommy, Ben, and Mike all standing at attention behind the patio table, napkins draped over their arms, ready to serve.

Both girls laughed. "Classic," said Parker. *Cult,* was the implied but unspoken second word of that statement.

Parker quizzed the three young guys over dinner. If she'd had more to drink at that point, she may have delved more deeply, but she kept her questions simple—hometowns, education, interests. Sutton had briefed her about them, and told her the sensitive topics to avoid for each. As Parker downed another glass of wine, she opened up about herself. She told them all about her wealthy, older husband who traveled all the time, her adult stepchildren, the fabulous trips she'd taken, and her famous friends. Parker's ability to go on and on about herself reminded Ben of Sutton, and he had to smile at the numerous similarities between the sisters.

After dinner, Alex suggested, "Tommy, why don't you take Parker and Sutton inside and show them your photography; Ben and Mike can help me clean up here."

"Yes, I'd like to see it," said Parker.

"Watch out, she has a fine arts degree and can be quite critical," warned Sutton.

"You wound me, my dear. I may be trained, but I still like what I like."

"Come on in," said Tommy.

On the coffee table, Tommy had arranged several photo albums and his iPad. He had produced eight-by-ten-inch photographic prints of many shots, and had many more in digital format. He began with the prints. First the architectural shots, then the human forms, which were a mix of both genders. Tommy had convinced classmates to pose for him, mostly nude. A mix of black-and-white and full color. Some were full-body shots, others were close-ups of faces, hands, torsos. What was striking was the lighting on all of them— lots of shadows and stark contrasts. Moody, but not depressing.

Sutton and Parker were both very quiet as they leafed through the pages of the albums.

Finally, Parker exclaimed, "Tommy, these are amazing."

"They truly are," agreed Sutton.

"You have quite an eye," added Parker. "Listen, Sutton knows magazine publishing, but I have friends in high places in the art publishing world. Would you be OK if I set up something for you to show your work to some of my friends? I think these could be—no, *should be*—published."

"Really?" asked Tommy excitedly.

While they were talking, the others had joined them.

"What's going on?" asked Alex.

"Parker thinks my photography could be publishable," Tommy said. "She wants to introduce me to her friends."

"Do it," urged Alex.

A cult leader probably wouldn't support that. She might have to admit she was wrong about him. Sutton would never let her live that down.

"But why don't I see any pictures of Mike here? I thought he was your primary subject. Besides, I was hoping to see one of you boys naked tonight."

Sutton pulled away Parker's wine glass. "That's enough vino for you, sister."

"Oh, I have those here," as Tommy picked up the iPad.

Only the underwear shots, Tom," Mike implored.

As Tommy scrolled through the progression of Mike's physical transformation, all in his black shorts, of course, Parker was surprised at how drastic the change had been. It was truly wonderful to watch this young man change from a skinny, frightened kid to the confident, handsome man she now saw standing beside her. And his backstory, made it even more compelling.

"You guys are doing something really cool here. I look forward to seeing it rolled out to the public.

"Thanks, Parker," Ben said, speaking for the group.

"I've got to get going."

They each hugged Parker goodbye. Hugging had been a discipline encouraged by Alex.

Standing at the door, Parker heard her name called. It was Tommy, out by the pool, naked. "Got your wish," he yelled, then jumped into the pool.

Ben said, "That's my boyfriend," and just shook his head.

Parker smiled, "Cute." It was a compliment.

And Sutton was surprised and impressed to see, Tommy, who she had always viewed as a skinny little boy, was actually a very ripped young man. *He might be magazine material,* she thought to herself. *We can always make him look taller, as we did with that sexy young politician.*

Moving to the car, Sutton asked Parker if she was OK to drive.

"Now who's being overprotective," came her sister's reply. "Put me in a room full of attractive men, I'm going to flirt. It has nothing to do with alcohol." They both laughed and Parker continued, "Listen, I'm sorry about what I said earlier. I can see why you're drawn to Alex and his guys. And I think this turnaround project is going to be big. I was really impressed with all of them, and their enthusiasm and commitment to the project and one another. You're the best at getting this in front of an audience. For the life of me, I don't understand why you still grovel to that asshole boss of yours anyway, staying at a job you've come to hate. Commit yourself to this."

She kissed Sutton's cheek and drove back to her big, empty house in Brentwood.

Sutton was overwhelmed by what Parker had just said to her. They'd always been close, but Parker had really struck a chord. Later in bed, as she and Alex lay there quietly, she continued to think about Parker's words, then about Alex and the guys, and then about what she needed to do.

CHAPTER 48

"Hi, Malcolm. It's Sutton. Good, good. How are you? Listen, I wanted to call you directly. I think you're making great moves here with the magazine. Kyle is doing very well in his role, and I think ready to take on even more responsibility. It's time for me to step aside and let him run with it. No, no, let me finish. We both know that keeping me on along with Kyle is costing too much money, so eventually you'd have to fire me. My contract calls for a large payout in the event of termination. I'm willing to leave peacefully with only a portion of that payout. You save the money on my salary now and a large payout later. It's really a good deal for you, and it allows me the time and flexibility to pursue some other endeavors. Don't worry, I'll abide by the restrictions in my contract. I'm not leaving for any competitor of the magazine. It's all good. I'm happy, and you save a ton of money. I'd like to retain my ownership stake, but if that's untenable, we can discuss a buyout there. Thanks for everything. My attorney is poised to call you tomorrow to work through the details of the separation. Have a great day, dear."

Malcolm never had a chance to speak. She didn't want to hear his false protests anyway. This is what he wanted, and it was too good of a deal for him to deny it.

Sutton took a deep breath. She'd never felt so free.

CHAPTER 49

True to her word, things with Emmy proceeded very slowly. Since Mike's romantic and very candid first date with her, they had gone to a movie—an action picture she'd chosen, as opposed to the rom-com he'd suggested. They'd also met for lunch and an afternoon bike ride on the beach promenade. Both dates had been fun, but he couldn't tell whether they were leading anywhere. To be fair, she'd also been traveling quite a bit in the last eight weeks, and they had had a few very long, long-distance phone conversations during that time. But still, he liked her and wanted to get to know her better. And with the confidence he had been building in his body and himself, he felt he deserved a little more attention from her.

And he'd admit, he was horny. His right hand had become all too good a friend, and he occasionally cheated on it with his left when Tommy and Ben were going at it in the room next to his. If Emmy didn't show him a little loving soon, he was going to have to start looking around. The problem was, his options were quite slim. School had yet to produce anyone of interest. And Ben didn't want him dating anyone from the gym, for fear of the *Project Mike* story getting out prematurely. They had even concocted a cover story about Mike being Tommy's cousin, getting buff to break into movies. It helped explain how this kid could afford the cost of daily training. And they'd regularly joke with the other actor wannabes that Mike's good looks, thick dick and lack of talent made him a perfect candidate for porn, which made the buff body even more important.

Mike decided to go for broke with Emmy. She had texted that she'd be "back in town Thursday" for a week, and "yes," she'd "love to get together" while she was home. He arranged with Alex and Tommy to *get lost* so that he could have the house to himself on Friday. He was going to invite Emmy to dinner—and hopefully more—at "his place."

Despite having been lauded for being the one who called, the invitation went by text due to the time zone difference. He didn't expect a reply until morning, but it came within a few minutes.

From Emmy: *Sounds like fun. Missing U.*

That was all the encouragement he needed to send his brain into overdrive.

Thursday had been the day for the latest progress photos, so he had a fresh spray tan, professional haircut, and beard trim. Now, what to wear? It was Friday afternoon, and Tommy was already gone, so he was on his own when it came to his outfit. Comfortable but sexy, if he could figure out what that was. Shorts were OK for a dinner at home, right? It was warm out, after all, and his legs were looking good. His slim fit, madras shorts hugged his ass and showed a nice bulge up front. A button up shirt would be too preppy so he chose a new body hugging tee he had just gotten. He was looking good and feeling better.

At a quarter past seven Friday evening, only fifteen minutes late, he heard the "Ding, dong, dong, ding, dong, ding, ding, dong." Alex was right—that doorbell had to go.

Mike met Emmy at the door. He had planned to be the aggressor, but she grabbed the front of his tee shirt and pulled him in for a long kiss. Suddenly his shorts were feeling even a little more snug.

"Well, hello there," he said as she drew herself away from his face.

Her hand was smoothing out the front of his shirt where she had grasped it as she said, "Sorry, I've been wanting to do that for a while. And this, too," she added as her hand ran up his chest.

Mike took her hand and pulled her though the door. He stood back and took a look at her. She was wearing a cropped silk top with spaghetti straps—mental note, no bra—and a long sarong-styled, patterned skirt with a slit up her left leg. He didn't know if he had hit the mark with the casual, sexy look, but she certainly had.

"You look amazing. Can I offer you a drink?"

"That sounds fantastic."

As he turned toward the kitchen, she grabbed his ass with her left hand and squeezed his butt cheek.

"I've been wanting to do that too."

This is going well, he thought.

They shared a bottle of chardonnay and only nibbled on the dinner he'd made. They were both too distracted to eat more.

"Let's go out and look at the stars," suggested Emmy. "Bring your glass."

With his hand in hers, she led him to the round daybed near the pool. There was a warm breeze drifting over the mountains. She hiked her skirt up a bit, so she could crawl onto the chaise, exposing nearly all her leg. Without being asked, he followed her. She set her glass on the side table, then took his to place there as well. As she turned back, he leaned in and kissed her. She lay back, and he covered her as they continued to kiss. He ran his hand down her arm to her side and onto her bare leg. She had one arm on his back, and the other, again, cupping his ass.

"Roll over on your back," she ordered.

He obeyed. She moved to straddle his crotch. The slit in the skirt was open wide enough now that he could see her panties.

"Sit up."

As he did, she pulled his tee shirt over his head. Then she pushed him back down. She was struck by how defined his pecs and abs had become. His dark chest hair was cropped short but still provided a nice contrast to his bronzed skin. She made mental comparison to Andre and wondered if she had a type. He looked so sexy. He had his hands on her thighs as she pulled her own top over her head, exposing her breasts.

"Wanna touch?"

He moved his hands toward her breasts.

"Not yet," she warned.

Next, she untied the knot that held up her shirt and tossed it aside. She scooted down the bed to unbuckle his belt and pull down his shorts. With Mike in only his boxer briefs and she in only panties, Emmy climbed back on top.

"OK, sexy man, now do whatever you want."

His hands went to her back and pulled her in for another deep kiss. He felt her breasts against his chest and wondered if his chest hair tickled her. Then he was rolling her over on her back. His left hand went to her right breast, and then his tongue was playing with the nipple. Her hands weren't idle— they had moved down under his briefs to feel his bare ass. Another mental comparison—smooth, unlike Andre. Then she was pulling the briefs down. She wanted them off. She wanted to see, and to feel and taste his cock. He was working on her panties, and she helped him get those off too. They were both naked together for the first time. He on his back and she on all fours. She admired his cock, stroked it with her hand a few times before guiding it into her mouth. The comparisons had stopped. She was now totally in the moment. Her smooth pussy was hovering over his face and he knew what to do. She sucked and moaned. He was breathing heavy as his tongue went to work.

"I want you," she cried. And in one seamless move, she twisted herself around to face him. He held her ass as she lowered herself on top.

"Condom," he tried to say. She covered his mouth with her hand. Neither lasted more than two minutes. They had been waiting too long for this. She came first. He then exploded inside of her and she hopped off to catch the straggling spurts in her mouth. She kissed him so he could taste his own cum. The warm, creamy liquid on his tongue flashed him back to his former life for just a moment, and he winced. Nothing else tasted like that. Then he was again back in the moment with Emmy. She collapsed on top of him with her leg wrapped over him, breathing heavily, heart still thumping. Her long hair fell across his face and the sweet smell of her shampoo contrasted with the muskiness of their sex-scented bodies. After a few minutes, she reached over for a wine glass and each took a sip. Then Mike pulled the cotton blanket over their still, naked bodies.

"So, tell me about your priors," Emmy said.

"What do you mean?"

"You've told me about selling yourself to guys…and your stepdad. I want to hear about your high school sweetheart. You know, your first time with a woman."

"My high school years were pretty fucked up." He tried to pause and let it stop there, but she prodded. "I mean, to distract myself from what was going on at home, I spent as much time at school as I could. I poured all my energy into my grades and praying that something would change at home. That my step dad would stay out of my room. I didn't date— didn't want to. Couldn't think about it. Then on the streets it was all about survival. I wasn't thinking about a relationship or sex, except to make some cash."

"Are you telling me I'm your first?"

"Woman, yes. Did I mess up? It felt right. It felt great."

"No, you were perfect. That's why I'm surprised."

"Anatomically it's not that different than with a guy. It's all friction and rhythm until you add emotion into the equation. Here, with you, I was doing what I wanted to be doing. For once."

She hugged him. "It's hard to imagine what you've been through."

"That's history. I'm so lucky and grateful for this new life. Thanks for being part of it." He kissed her above the eye.

There was a long pause, then he continued, "I'm surprised you didn't let me get a condom. For the record, Alex had me get tested a couple of times since I've been here, and I'm clean. Have you been tested? I mean, you were sleeping with Andre. Who knows where his dick has been."

"No, I'm clean too. Regular testing. I'm allergic to latex, so…"

"Oh. Good, we're both healthy."

Another long pause.

"I'm glad our paths crossed. Right here in this house. I credit Andre," joked Emmy.

"Yeah, the asshole was good for something."

They both laughed.

"By the way, he's got nothing on you in bed." One last comparison, the only one verbalized.

He squeezed her tight. "Thanks for being my first."

In the weeks that followed, there were many more nights together, both in his room at the house and at her apartment. He frightened her from time to time when, while sleeping, he'd begin thrashing about. He assured her that the shrink said it was normal, as he was still having flashbacks to the abuse by his stepdad and also the trauma of the stabbings.

"It will subside in time," was his promise.

About a month later, she officially declared herself his "girlfriend" to the guys, which in her words, meant exclusive. She even began acknowledging her "boyfriend Mike" in interviews. He was still under wraps, so the media and audience were left wondering about the mysterious Mike who was dating one of the country's top, up-and-coming models.

CHAPTER 50

As much as Mike liked Emmy, his insecurities sometimes got the better of him. Her world was more glamorous than he could imagine, while his consisted of the gym and school. And he didn't even want to think about how different their pasts were. Could their relationship really work?

"Hey, I have an idea. Can you get away next weekend for a couple of days?" Mike asked Emmy over the phone.

"That sounds like fun. What do you have in mind?"

"Let's take the motorcycle up the coast to Santa Barbara. Stay at a bed and breakfast. Hit a winery or two. Talk."

It felt like a test. Could the city girl survive for a weekend with just what she could carry on a motorcycle? She was up to that challenge. "OK, the winery put me over the top," she laughed.

A few days later, Emmy, wearing jeans, boots, and a black leather jacket, was throwing her leg over the back of Mike's shiny blue Yamaha. Her long black hair was tied back in a ponytail, to avoid the windblown mess she would get in Andre's convertible. The helmet slid on easily over it. Gold-rimmed Ray Ban aviators and the red backpack completed her look. Mike wore his pack on his chest so Emmy could hold on to him tight and he could feel her warm body against his. His leather jacket smelled new as she buried her face in his back. Her hands snuck up under the waistband of the jacket to keep them warm against the white tee shirt covering his flat stomach.

It was slow-going through Malibu, but once they hit the 101, they made it to their destination in a couple of hours. The old Victorian house sat on a hill surrounded by grape vines planted in neat rows. The scent of the ripening grapes filled the air as it wafted off the breeze from the distant ocean on the horizon.

"Smell that," said Emmy. "Makes me want a glass of wine."

"Then let's get checked in and get you to the tasting room."

Throughout the afternoon and evening, they laughed and told stories as they tried rosés and reds. Then they had an early dinner before retiring to their room. The queen-size, wrought iron bed sat up high off the floor. The fireplace in the corner cast a warm glow on the walls. Outside the window was pitch black.

Lying next to each other in bed, she wore the tee shirt he'd had on all day. She loved how it smelled. He wore only his underwear and pulled the fluffy comforter up over his shoulder as the fire worked to take the chill from the night air. Her hand stroked his chest hair under the covers.

"So your year is almost up. *Project Mike* is about to launch. What happens next with you?"

"That's a good question. I haven't really talked with Ben about it. School will be my focus, I guess. It's looking like I'll get accepted to UCLA, and Alex has offered to continue to fund my tuition—I told him it would only be a loan. Parker and Sutton are telling me to write a book about the *Project Mike* experience from my perspective, so that's a possibility,

I guess. I don't know, I've got all these options I've never had before. And this past year has been so structured, I'm a little nervous about having to figure things out on my own."

"Well, the nice thing is you've still got these guys as great friends. And I'm sure Tommy has no shortage of advice for you."

They both giggled at Tommy's expense.

"What about you? Any changes coming for you?" His hand was now resting on her bare hip, the waistband of her thong under his fingers.

"Tomorrow. I'm tired; let's just go to sleep now." Her eyes were heavy. He kissed her forehead, then her lips. She rolled over with her back to him, and pushed herself up tight against him. His arm around her stomach.

A rooster crowed and they both opened their eyes to yellow rays streaming through the window. The sun through the old glass made a whimsical pattern on the wall. The once glowing embers were now just gray ash.

"Good morning," came from Emmy first.

Mike pulled her in for a deep kiss. "Sorry about the breath," he said.

"Hey, I won't complain if you don't." She initiated the second kiss of the day, then reached down into his shorts, delighted to find that he was already hard. Her head dove under the covers. For the next hour they played with each other, bringing each nearly to climax before backing off and starting over again. When they were done, they showered together in the old claw-foot tub and marveled in their reflection coming from the rapidly steaming gilt-edged mirror. They kissed again, a pattern that would repeat many times throughout the day.

"Welcome to Brickyard Cellars," said the young woman. "Are you interested in white or red?"

Emmy looked up at Mike and said, "Yes." They both laughed.

As they sampled the selection of wines the woman was offering, Emmy said to Mike, "So you asked what my plans were. I'd like your opinion."

He held up his glass, "A little too sweet for my taste."

Emmy slapped his arm, "No, I'm serious."

"Sorry." He recoiled, laughing. "So tell me."

"I want to quit modeling." She took a deep breath. "That felt good to say. I've got some ideas I've wanted to pursue for a long time. But a few days ago, a girlfriend from college called me. She runs a small fashion house in Manhattan. She told me if I ever want to put my degree to work I should come join her. It's really tempting." She took a sip of her wine. "It would mean moving to New York. What do you think?"

A number of things were running through Mike's mind—not the least of which was that Andre was in New York. Mike took her hand and looked into her eyes. "I'm not sure I can answer that. But I can ask you some questions to help you consider the options. It's an exercise I learned in school to evaluate things."

"Like what?"

"Do you know what your role would be? What are the ideas you've wanted to pursue? Do you like New York enough to live there? When do you have to decide? Can you do both— join your friend and still pursue your ideas?" Mike pounded her with a barrage of these and more questions. She took it all in, answered what she could and acknowledged what she hadn't thought of on her own. They were continually interrupted with a new wine to sample.

"Let's get out of here and find a bar where we can talk," Mike offered. They thanked the sommelier, and when they found a nearby bar, spent the rest of the afternoon exploring Emmy's options.

One more night in the big wrought iron bed that squeaked whenever they moved. Emmy again in his tee shirt.

"So, I never answered your question," said Mike. "I put you off because I wanted time to think about it. But I listened carefully to everything you told me, and I have an opinion…if you still want it."

"Well, yeah. Of course I want it." She pinched his nipple, making him flinch.

"Oww," he said, rubbing it. "Well, if you're going to abuse me, I think you should move. Get the hell out of here. Move to the Big Apple."

A pause. She looked at him, surprised.

"Here's my real opinion. You don't want to move to New York. You don't want to jump into something that someone else has built. You should make a name for yourself. Build your own brand. I think you've got the energy, and I know you've got the smarts." Mike's head was propped up on his hand while his other hand played with Emmy's fingers. "I've learned a ton from Sutton and Alex about finding an audience. Maybe you and I…um…maybe you and I could do this together. I mean, I want to finish school but…"

She untangled her hand from his and reached over to stroke his furry cheek.

"I don't want to leave you," she said.

"Then don't."

"Thanks for telling me how you feel. Now it's time for me to think. I'll decide in the next few days. But I'm pretty sure I know what I'm going to do."

Looking at each other in the flickering light from the fireplace, they were quiet. Finally, Mike spoke, "There's something else I want to tell you."

After another long pause, "I love you." No hesitation. No screaming it during the passion of sex. Just a sincere statement that received a soft, "I love you, too," in return.

At breakfast, before heading back to the city, Mike began to speak. "I had a bad dream last night."

"I know, I felt you tense up."

"I dreamed that none of this ever happened to me. That Ben didn't find me. That I never met Tommy or Alex...or you. I was a forty-year-old man, dirty, angry, and digging through garbage cans looking for anything I could find to eat or sell. I am having such difficulty reconciling how I made it out. Why was I the lucky one? What can I do help others?"

"You're a good man, Mike. You'll find a way to help.

CHAPTER 51

Alex and Maggie were once again perched on a cliff near the top at Runyon Canyon. He had worked up a sweat on the climb, but the overcast sky provided little sunlight for warmth and, in his wet tee shirt, he began to shiver. For some reason, the piano track from Springsteen's *Thunder Road* was playing over and over in his head. It was quiet on the cliff that day so he pulled Maggie close and said aloud, "What are we going to do, girl? This can't last like this forever. Our guys are all going to head their own way. They have their lives to lead. Tommy and Ben need to start their own household as a family, whether it's just the two of them or, maybe they decide to have kids. And Mike, shit, he's got his whole life ahead of him. He needs to explore who he's going to be. I need to kick them out of the house…launch them like a mother bird.

"But shit, it's going to be lonely, here. You and I have both come to really appreciate the energy, the noise, the pure joy they bring to the house." Continuing his conversation with Maggie, he said, "Oh, I suspect that they'll still come around when they can. It just won't be the same. Is this what parents feel like when their kids leave home? We know it's right, but we feel sorry for ourselves?" He was tearing up a bit now.

Missing all the noise was what he feared the most. All his life, he'd noticed different sounds as he was falling asleep. They always gave him a sense of where he was at that moment. Over the years, hearing those same sounds would bring him back to that moment in time. Whether it was their chatter in the living room, the garage door opening after a late night out, or a midnight refrigerator raid, he knew whenever he'd hear similar noises again, he'd be taken back to this wonderful, joyful period of his life.

But that would be reminiscing. *Stop that! I don't do that.* Then his mind shifted to his definition of heaven and hell. He wasn't religious, but he knew they existed. Oh, not as places you go when you die. No, hell could exist right here. And it wasn't the devil, with pitchforks and fire. It was loneliness. That's the only tough situation you can never escape on your own. It always requires someone else. And heaven? Sure, there was life after death, but it's not sitting on a cloud wearing wings and strumming a harp. It's living on through the people and generations you influenced, impacted, and loved while alive.

Shifting his mind back to the question at hand. "What about Andre? No, that's over. He's on a very different path and not very good for me. As sexy as he is, I always feel worse about myself after being with him. I'm glad he's kicked the drugs, though."

"And Sutton? She's the opposite of Andre. Oh, she's as sexy as him, don't get me wrong on that. Even without his big dick." Alex chuckled to himself. "But I feel like she brings out the best in me. And she doesn't push me to be someone other than who I am. How can you not love that?"

He took a deep breath. "As I see it, we have a few options. One of them is to leave this town and check out somewhere new. Or we can go home. Can we still call Minnesota home? I guess. We do still have a house there…and friends. But I like it here. I like the weather, I like the attitude. And I sure don't want to add any obstacles to staying connected with our young friends. And honestly, I really don't want to leave Sutton." His mind went to a memory of the noise of her heels on the floor at their first meeting.

"So I guess there's only one option. And it's a good option. Just not one I thought I'd ever pursue again. But it's you and me girl. We're a team, and I don't make a decision like this without your buy-in. What do you say, do you agree?"

Maggie looked away from the gray horizon and up at her loving master, then licked his cheek in approval of whatever he was saying. Blind trust in the man who had rescued her from that shelter so many years ago and given her a loving home, just as he had with the guys. He had her approval.

Later that evening, the clouds from the day were now producing a steady rain. Alex was home alone. The house was quiet as he sat on the couch with a glass of wine, staring at dancing flames in the fireplace and listening to the raindrops hit the pool water outside the open patio doors. Another sound on which to reminisce.

"I'm home," called Tommy as he came through the door. Alex heard the keys hit the bowl by the door and then saw Tommy enter the room.

"Where've you been?" queried Alex.

"Tonight's Carole's big award dinner. I've been over there helping her and Ben get ready. Ben's her date, you know. They looked great, if I do say so myself. Here, I took a picture of them in the limo."

"Good for them. She looks so happy. That was really nice of Ben to escort her. But they must have left hours ago, what have you been doing since?"

"Oh, I've just been driving around in the rain. Thinking about shit. Is there any wine left?"

"Yeah. The bottle is in the kitchen. Grab a glass."

Glass in hand, Tommy joined Alex and Maggie on the massive couch. Maggie was on Alex's right, so Tommy lay down next to her, with his head on her chest. Alex continued to stroke Maggie's fur and Tommy's hair in the same motion.

"So where were you all afternoon?" asked Tommy.

"Maggie and I hiked up Runyon. I got kind of chilled, so I came back here for a hot shower and the fire."

"Runyon is your thinking place. Any great thoughts you want to share? Revelations maybe?"

"I just had to think through what it's going to be like around here without you guys. Mike's ready to launch, and you and Ben must be planning what you two do next."

Maggie was panting. Too warm. She moved to the rug near the open door. Tommy scooted over and put his head in Alex's lap while Alex continued to stare at the fire. Tommy rolled onto his back and looked up at Alex.

"You sound like you're reminiscing. Isn't that against your rules?"

"Yeah, I kind of fell off the wagon today. Maybe too much wine. But I'm looking at the future, too. And right now I'm just enjoying this moment here with you."

"Ben and I have talked about getting our own place, but that doesn't mean we won't be hanging out here all the time. We're not breaking up like The Beatles…or One Direction."

"Yeah, you're right. The rain just makes me melancholy." Alex didn't believe what either he or Tommy was saying. He knew the boys were all entering a new phase of their lives. It reminded him of a line from a movie. *Where you're going, I've already been.* He thought it but didn't say it. And he wasn't really melancholy; he just wasn't ready to talk about his own plans yet.

"Don't be sad, Ax. You're not losing us."

Alex looked down at Tommy and smiled. He looked back at the fire. His right hand resting on Tommy's stomach moved up and down with each breath Tommy took.

After a while, Tommy was dozing. Alex nudged him saying, "I need to go to bed so I'm not a wreck tomorrow. You do, too."

Twenty minutes later, Tommy was standing in the doorway of Alex's room, his silhouette barely visible.

"Ax, you awake?" whispered Tommy.

"Yeah, what's up?"

"It's too quiet over there. Can I sleep with you?"

"Are you feeling kind of melancholy now?"

"Yeah, a little, I guess."

"OK, but just sleep. And you're wearing shorts?"

"Just for you." Tommy laughed quietly.

"Come on."

Alex rolled on his side and Tommy crawled into the big bed behind Alex wrapping his arm around Alex's chest. For a little guy, Tommy made a very good "big spoon."

Chapter 52

Ben and Mike made the round of radio talk shows scheduled by Sutton. Then there were the fluff afternoon TV shows. The real coup in their eyes, though, was when they were booked for six minutes in the last half hour of a national morning news broadcast. Sutton was in the green room, while Ben and Mike sat at the Plexiglas table with the hosts. They were reviewing the before and after photos, talking about the process and what it meant, and finally, discussing the backgrounds and hardships of both Ben and Mike.

"Tell us about the media you've covered."

Ben shared the magazine series and website, which made money. And the upcoming book.

Sutton's phone vibrated.

From Ax: *Good job, babe. Our boys are doing great. Love U. Ax*

He was watching the program from their hotel room a few blocks away in Times Square.

To Ax: *Will U B joining us for lunch?*

From Ax: *Yes, but I may be a little late. I have something I need to take care of while I'm here. I'll let you know when I'm on my way.*

"So I want to understand this. Sorry to refer to you in the third person, Mike," the anchor said, turning her attention back to Ben, "You took a homeless kid and with the help of investors sent him to college and gave him a new life. Why go through the whole fitness piece? He's studying for a career in business."

"Well, my passion is fitness." Ben was talking now. "And I felt I could learn a lot about the human body's response to nutrition and exercise in this very focused, practical case study. And, I wanted the business model to be sustainable. I have investors, not donors. I needed a way to monetize this and pay them back. If the money raised had been a donation, it would help one kid. This way the money is available to be reinvested, one way or another, and we got to tell a pretty interesting story in the process."

"And my girlfriend likes the new physique quite a lot," joked Mike. The group chuckled and a host interjected, "That's right, we should mention you're dating model Emmy Ayn. Not bad." They'd finally gone public only days before.

The broadcast was drawing to an end. Sutton's guys had done well. They concluded the segment with, "Well, that's awesome. And Mike, you look great."

"That's it. I'm next. Sign me up!" The news anchor turned back to the camera. "Our time is up, have a great day, and a great weekend."

Alex exited the elevator on the 34th floor and walked into the New York offices of Ocariz Architects. He was happy Andre had agreed to see him.

The receptionist led him to Andre's massive office. Andre stood in front of a wall of windows with the skyscrapers of Manhattan as a backdrop. An elegant businessman. So different from the sexy young guy at the beach with his surfboard. Andre looked happy, but Alex knew he could never be as happy in this world as when he was riding a wave. He also knew that, for Andre, family loyalty trumped everything.

Alex extended his hand, but Andre opened his arms and wrapped them around Alex in a big hug, then kissed him on both cheeks, as his Italian family would. "Too much time has passed my friend. And I do consider you my friend. Thank you for helping me clean up my act by telling me what I needed to hear."

"I'm glad things are going well for you, and that we can be friends."

"I saw the interview on TV this morning; it looks like your investment is paying off. Congratulations. I'm sorry for being a jerk about it."

"We like to call you 'the asshole' as it relates to that." Alex chuckled.

"Fair enough." Andre smiled and nodded.

"But, apology accepted. Thank you, I'll pass it on to the guys."

"Please do. I wish everyone well. Now, what brings you by this morning? Just a friendly visit while in town?"

"Not much more than that. But I do have a favor to ask."

"Certainly."

"I know you and Emmy have stayed in touch, and I understand you're moving to London permanently. Is that right?"

"Yes, I'll always care for Emmy and am delighted she's found happiness with your Mike. And the move is true. It's necessary for the business."

"And that you've closed up the beach house but aren't selling it right now."

"That's right. It's not a good time to sell, and if I can get back there in a couple of years…In the meantime, the surf in France and Portugal will do."

"Well, I'd like to rent it from you for a year. You name the price. I'm sure you'll be reasonable about it."

"You want to rent my little beach house? You could have any property you wanted."

"It's not for me."

"Oh, you have a boy toy you want to keep hidden from your fiancé."

"Something like that."

Taking a key off of his ring, he handed it to Alex. "Here my friend. It's yours for the next year."

"You don't have…"

"No, it's the least 'the asshole' can do. Enjoy. Our little secret."

"Thank you, Andre. I take back all the nasty things I said about you."

"They were all deserved, I'm sure. I'll have my aide, Bryce, reach out to you about the contacts for maintenance, etc."

Now, Alex hugged Andre and kissed his cheeks. "I really did enjoy our time together. I wish you well in London, my friend." Alex held him tight…for the last time.

"Thank you. As did I," replied Andre. "And congratulations on your engagement. She's a lucky woman to have gotten you."

"Thank you." Holding up the key, he said, "I've got to run. Thanks again." Alex turned and exited the office.

After lunch, the crew loaded into the chauffeured Escalade and headed to JFK. "Let's get home," said Alex. "We have a birthday to celebrate."

CHAPTER 53

On the flight back to LA, Ben and Tommy sat next to each other in First Class, with Mike across the aisle listening to his headphones. Alex and Sutton were two rows back.

Ben turned to Tommy, "I guess I need to figure out where Mike's going to live, now. The year with Alex is almost up, you and I are moving into our own place. I'm sure Sutton's going to want her privacy when she moves in."

"Technically, that's not your problem," replied Tommy. "He's a big boy. You've gotten him on his feet. He's famous. He wants to focus on his education now that he's been accepted at UCLA. Maybe he wants to shack up with Emmy."

"You're right. I've got to initiate the conversation though. He's been spending so much time with her and his school work, he doesn't even know our plans. Hell, have you even told Alex?"

"Yes, we chatted." Tommy didn't share any more details of the chat. "What about Carole? Have you talked to her?"

"Yes, I have. She's completely supportive. Frankly, I think I spend so little time there that she's happy to be rid of me so she can rent my room to someone she can take care of. She wants you and Mike to come over for a farewell dinner though."

"Cool. Can I request her lasagna?"

"I'll make the suggestion. Now back to Mike."

"You want me to do it? I'll get him drunk and then tell him."

"Very funny."

Mike was engrossed in his textbook and enjoying his music, oblivious to what was going on next door.

Saturday night, Mike was picking Emmy up for dinner. When he got to her apartment, she met him at the door with a wrapped box.

"What's going on?" he asked.

"Happy Birthday, sweetie. Let's go. It's a surprise."

As she pulled out of her garage, she instructed him to open the box. Inside he found a blindfold.

"Put it on," she instructed.

"I guess it's a good thing you're driving."

Because he was familiar with the route back to Alex's, she drove around in an attempt to disguise where they were headed.

"Are you driving back to my place? Is there a surprise party? Is that why Tommy was acting so weird today?"

"I'm not saying, but you'd better act surprised."

"*Oui*, mademoiselle," and a mock salute.

She helped him through the door, still blindfolded.

"OK, take it off."

As expected, the moment he lifted the mask, came a thunderous, "Surprise."

He scanned the room, Tommy and Ben and Alex and Sutton, of course, and even Parker. Emmy was at his side and over to the left, Carole. How sweet. "Man, you got me. Here I thought Emmy was taking me to some kinky sex club...and I was right!"

They all laughed. Tommy and Ben came up on either side of him, wrapped arms around him and started giving noogies.

"Happy Birthday, Buddy!"

He turned left and kissed Tommy on the cheek and right to kiss Ben.

Tommy put his hand to his face and said, "I'll never wash this cheek again. How about kissing this one," pointing to his own ass.

Mike pushed them both away, laughing. Last year he was huddled in a corner alone, trying to stay warm and out of sight. *Look at me now,* he thought, *with such wonderful friends. I truly am the luckiest guy in the world.*

Alex came up. "Go say hi to Carole, then I have a little surprise for you."

He gave Carole a big hug, "Thanks so much for being here." He hugged her again.

"You've come a long way, Mike. I know I had little to do with it, but I'm proud of you, my boy."

Mike's eyes welled, up. "What are you talking about? You gave me the first soft bed I'd had in years. Sure, I had to share it with Ben, but…" They both laughed at Ben's expense. "Carole, you let a dirty kid from the streets into your house. That could have dangerous. Don't do that again."

"Well, when you put it that way, let's say I'm glad we're all still alive."

"Speaking of that, Ax, do we have some champagne or something?" Mike was taking the floor.

"Why yes, in fact we do. It's right here and already open. I was going to make a toast."

"Sorry to steal your thunder, dad. And I mean that in the good way, not the you-want-to-fuck-me way. But I have a toast to make." He knew his past was behind him and could now joke about it. He waited while Alex poured champagne for everyone then continued. "I have to go chronologically or I'll get confused. This is off-the-cuff, so cut me some slack and don't interrupt."

"Is he stoned?" Tommy whispered to Ben.

"No, I think he's just excited. Adrenaline. most likely."

"First, Ben…" Then Carole, then Alex, Tommy, Sutton, Emmy. Mike talked about what each of them had done for him and meant to him. Then he closed with, "Seriously, without each of you and all of you, I'd be dead. I promise, I won't let this life you saved go to waste. I love each of you individually, and all of you collectively. You've redefined the meaning of family for me. You're the best family I could ever imagine."

Tears flowed around the room.

Alex composed himself and stepped forward. He hugged Mike and held him in the embrace for several seconds. Mike hugged back just as hard, then whispered so only Alex could hear, "I wish you were my real dad."

Sobbing, Alex replied, "As far as I'm concerned, I am. You're all my sons, and I'll always be here for you." Tommy and Ben joined the hug. The four women held hands and were in tears as well. Finally, they released the embrace and Alex stepped back. He reached into his pocket and began to speak to Mike and the group.

Wiping away tears, "Mike, you've come a long way in this past year. You've blessed all our lives by being part of it. Your loyalty, commitment, and humor make you a truly wonderful human being. I have little present for you on your twenty-third birthday."

Out of his pocket came a rabbit's foot on a chain. Alex opened his hand to expose the key that was attached to it.

"You're poised to break out on your own. The next year will be a lot more development for you as you continue on with your schooling and decide how you're going to live your life. I've gotten you your own place for the next year so you're free to experience life on your own terms. Good luck, my son."

Mike was stunned. The group applauded and cried out, "Hear, hear."

The two hugged again, and then the rest joined in.

"More champagne," called Alex as he made his way around the room to refill glasses.

CHAPTER 54

Tommy was sitting on Mike's bed as he dressed for class.

"So, Ben and I are moving in together. Are you going to ask Emmy to move into the beach house with you?"

"No, I don't think either of us is quite ready for that yet. I need to know what it's like to be on my own, albeit a lot different than the last time I was. You've all taught me a lot; now I need to teach myself some things. I'm looking forward to getting to know myself in this new life."

"Tommy, Mike," came a call from the living room. "Come out here; Sutton has news."

They came into the living room to see Sutton shaking with excitement.

"Tommy, Parker got a call this morning from the publishing people you met with last month. They want to publish a collection of your photographs. This is huge. They produce spectacular coffee-table books and have some of the best distribution channels."

Mike hugged Tommy from behind. Being several inches taller, he rested his chin on Tommy's head as Tommy stood there stunned.

Sutton continued, "So Tommy, what do you think? Are you in?"

"Well, I don't know, I'll have to check with my lawyer." A pause and a laugh, then, "Hell yeah!"

Tommy turned around, hugging Mike back, and they jumped up and down together. Mike whispered, "Any shots of me better be wearing at least underwear."

Tommy faked a brotherly knee to Mike's groin. "We'll see."

He moved to hug Sutton, and then pulled Alex into the hug as well.

"I can't wait to tell Ben...and my parents. And I guess this proves that 'it *is* who you know.'" He laughed.

CHAPTER 55

Mike returned to the beach house from Emmy's after midnight. He'd been living there a couple of weeks and was still getting settled in. As he rode his motorcycle toward the driveway, he was daydreaming and thinking about getting a pet. *A dog maybe. A rescue, like Maggie, would be great.* But with his school schedule maybe a cat would be better. He also told himself he needed to try surfing again. *Maybe this time I can stand up on the damn board. If Andre could do it, I should be able to. How about a tattoo? But of what? And where? Definitely need to think about that one.* As he rounded the corner, he saw a lump up against the wall where he had slept just a year earlier.

He tucked the bike into the garage, and Mike grabbed his old blanket that Andre had stashed there. He walked over to the figure, standing next to it. He could see it was a young man, probably a couple of years younger than himself.

In a soft voice, he said, "Hi, I'm Mike. Are you cold? How about a blanket? Are you hungry? Do you want to talk?"

The figure moved faster than Mike could imagine. He only caught the glimmer of the blade under the street light before it entered his chest and everything went black.

CHAPTER 56

Alex was sitting across the Lucite table from the three news anchors, who were questioning him.

"First," came from one of the hosts, "I know it's been a year, but our condolences. We really enjoyed meeting Mike. He was such a nice young man with so much ahead of him. We're really sad that he's no longer with us."

"Thank you," came Alex's reply.

There was a second "Thank you." This one from Ben, who was seated next to him.

"He had such a bright future ahead of him," the anchor continued.

Alex interrupted, "See, that's the thing—all these kids should have a future they're looking forward to, instead of living day-to-day. A lot of them die under questionable circumstances, without any attention. It's kind of a victimless crime to many people. Mike's death was one of the few that even made the news. Not because of where he came from, but because of who he'd become. He wanted to help these kids, and his death did a lot to raise attention to the issue."

Alex took a much needed breath, "Sorry, as you can tell, I can get worked up about this issue quite easily."

"No problem, but you say that not all these kids are in trouble."

"That's true. Some are just what we call vagabonding."

"Vagabonding?" Alex was interrupted with the question.

"Yeah. These kids aren't desperate. They're wandering, trying to figure things—and themselves—out. Sometimes they sleep on the street, or they're couch-surfing. They're finding free food. But at the end of the day, they have a family to go back to at some point. But it's still dangerous. And they need safe places to go in the meantime. And it's not just LA. In the winter, they tend to migrate to southern states. In the summer, every city sees this." Alex was getting excited by the opportunity to educate the audience.

Now the second anchor turned to Ben while Alex calmed himself.

"Now Ben, when you were here with Mike last time, you had just completed *Project Mike* and were working on a book documenting it, which has now been released. Tell us about that."

"That's right. After Mike was killed," he swallowed hard every time he used that word, "we considered abandoning the idea out of respect for him. But after discussing it at length, we realized that Mike had put so much effort into the project that we needed to share it. Share his results…to honor him."

"It must have been hard to relive it with him gone."

"Sure, but in some ways, writing the book reminded me of just how great it was getting to know him and see him change. See him be happy with what he was doing with his life. He wanted to help others. Others like him. The message of the book can help those who want to get in shape, and the proceeds from the book are going to help other at-risk kids like Alex was talking about."

"We met Sutton when she was here with you last year, and I know she's in the green room today. How's she doing?"

"She's an incredibly strong woman," replied Alex. "I credit her with helping us all work through the pain. She's been very nurturing. And now she's working on a book. She's exploring how older kids and young adults perceive the world differently. Not just as a matter of the times, but a more timeless look at the stage of life. Sixteen to twenty-two-year-olds are often viewed as troubled or temperamental, even aimless, but really that's one of the most free times in a person's life. Think about it—they should see nothing but opportunity. And it impacts their view on everything from careers to relationships, and it's why they're so unbound by conventions. She's working with psychologists, behaviorists, and others to describe that phenomenon."

"Wow, that's a different perspective on things. And what about Emmy? We never met her, but it feels like we know her."

"Losing Mike was really rough for her, as you can imagine. Being around us is too difficult for her right now. She went to London, and Andre is helping her move on. He turned out to be a good guy after all. Mike brought out the best in all of us."

A second host chimed in. "Ben's book is titled, Project Mike, but there's also a second book that you've written, Alex, that also bears that title. What's going on there?"

"Yes, yes. Ben wrote the book that was intended all along. His book describes the clinical and emotional process of taking Mike from desperate to determined. And he did a really good job. Everyone should read it." Alex took a brief pause before continuing.

Sutton and Tommy were watching the large monitor in the green room. They both leaned forward anxiously waiting to hear his next words.

"But I saw a different story. Honestly, I'm not sure it would have come to me if Mike hadn't died, but it's a story that could have, should have been told, even if he was still here. I started writing it as therapy but quickly realized it was just so logical. This was an important story to tell, how we all came together as a family. An unconventional family by most standards, but the true definition of a family. It's the story of us. It's a love story."

Alex held up the book to the camera.

On the cover, the title: *PROJECT MIKE, A Love Story.*

— THE END —

A note from the author:

The character of Michael was inspired by a young man who sought assistance from a homeless youth program I volunteered with for several months in 2015. He was very quiet, kept to himself, and I never learned his name. After several weeks attending the Sunday arts and meal program, he disappeared and never returned. His story was pieced together from those of other young men and women who were regular attendees of the same program—the struggles that brought them there, and the perils they faced on the street. I wish this mysterious young man well, and pray that his ultimate fate plays out differently than the fictional character Michael.